MURDER IN HASTE
Mike Shayne's 40th Case
BRETT HALLIDAY

WHO'D EVER THINK that things would reach such a pass in Miami that Mike Shayne would come to the rescue of his arch-enemy, Peter Painter?

Well, that's the situation when the dapper chief of detectives of Miami Beach plays things just a little too close to his chest this time, concealing vital information that might clear a convicted murderer until the very last moment before his execution to cash in on the publicity value; and then getting himself kidnapped by a ruthless gang of killers who are determined to keep him out of circulation until an innocent man is electrocuted.

Mike Shayne *really* doesn't care whether Painter comes out of it alive or not (though he does realize that life would lose some of its savor if there were no Peter Painter for him to needle), but he is concerned about a miscarriage of justice . . . egged on by the lovely and willing wife of the accused man, and the lovely and not-unwilling widow of the victim.

Ironically enough, it takes a bomb thrown into the hospital room of a paralyzed man (occupied by Shayne) and the deliberate sinking of a luxury cruiser in the waters of Biscayne Bay (with Painter trapped below decks) to bring this fast-paced story to an exciting and unpredictable climax.

This country's toughest private eye, and Miami's most-publicized citizen has never been in a tighter spot or fought his way against greater odds.

BRETT HALLIDAY *also wrote*

DIVIDEND ON DEATH
THE PRIVATE PRACTICE OF MICHAEL SHAYNE
THE UNCOMPLAINING CORPSES
TICKETS FOR DEATH
BODIES ARE WHERE YOU FIND THEM
MICHAEL SHAYNE TAKES OVER
THE CORPSE CAME CALLING
MURDER WEARS A MUMMER'S MASK
BLOOD ON THE BLACK MARKET
MICHAEL SHAYNE'S LONG CHANCE
MURDER AND THE MARRIED VIRGIN
MURDER IS MY BUSINESS
MARKED FOR MURDER
BLOOD ON BISCAYNE BAY
COUNTERFEIT WIFE
MICHAEL SHAYNE'S TRIPLE MYSTERY
BLOOD ON THE STARS
A TASTE FOR VIOLENCE
CALL FOR MICHAEL SHAYNE
THIS IS IT, MICHAEL SHAYNE
FRAMED IN BLOOD
WHEN DORINDA DANCES
WHAT REALLY HAPPENED
ONE NIGHT WITH NORA
SHE WOKE TO DARKNESS
DEATH HAS THREE LIVES
STRANGER IN TOWN
THE BLONDE CRIED MURDER
WEEP FOR A BLONDE
SHOOT THE WORKS
MURDER AND THE WANTON BRIDE
FIT TO KILL
DATE WITH A DEAD MAN
TARGET: MIKE SHAYNE
DIE LIKE A DOG
MURDER TAKES NO HOLIDAY
DOLLS ARE DEADLY
THE HOMICIDAL VIRGIN
KILLERS FROM THE KEYS

MURDER IN HASTE

new MIKE SHAYNE *novel*

BRETT HALLIDAY

A TORQUIL BOOK

Distributed by
DODD, MEAD & COMPANY
NEW YORK

© COPYRIGHT 1961 BY BRETT HALLIDAY
ALL RIGHTS RESERVED
Library of Congress Catalog Card Number 61-12380

A condensed version of this book was published in
ARGOSY MAGAZINE

All the characters in this book are fictitious, and any resemblance to actual persons, living or dead, is purely coincidental.

PRINTED IN THE UNITED STATES OF AMERICA
BY THE COLONIAL PRESS INC.

Dedicated to "CHIPS"

The Terror of N. Frederic Street

1

AS THE POWERFUL radio-equipped Cadillac slowed for the exit onto one of the smallest of the Bay Harbor islands, Chief-of-Detectives Peter Painter leaned forward and told his driver to shut off the siren. He was calling on a lady, and he thought it might be considered bad taste to arrive with his siren wailing. The neighbors might think she was being arrested.

He removed a cigarette from his filter holder and crushed it in the back-seat ashtray as the Cadillac drifted to a stop before a rambling stucco house. There was another Cadillac in the driveway, this one a white convertible. The rear lawn sloped off gently to a private dock and a boathouse.

Painter got out, giving the back of his jacket a smart tug to get rid of wrinkles. "Now don't just sit there," he told Heinemann, his driver. "Move around. Stay under cover and keep your eyes open."

"Sure, Chief," Heinemann said. He was a short, balding detective with overlong arms and grease-blackened fingernails. "How do I move around and stay under cover at the same time? And it might help if I knew what I was supposed to keep my eyes open for."

Painter, always on the alert for signs of insubordination, shot him a sharp look and started for the house. But he turned back.

"You've got a point there," he admitted. "You don't want to be taken by surprise. I have reason to believe that somebody may try to take a shot at me. If it does happen, it won't be a crackpot operation. It'll be a professional job all the way.

That's why I think we're all right here—there's only the one exit off the island. But that's no excuse for goofing off."

"No, sir," Heinemann said, leaving on the parking lights and sliding out from behind the wheel. "Because if there's any shooting, I'm right here in the line of fire."

"And remember that."

Satisfied with the set of his jacket and the position of his necktie, Painter went up the front walk to the house, coming down too hard on his heels, as he invariably did. He was a short man, and to get the most out of his limited stature he held himself as erect as a bow-string. His shoes with their extra-thick heels were highly polished. He wore made-to-measure suits, and in the opinion of his numerous critics, he was usually somewhat over-dressed for his job.

He sounded the bell, and rearranged his breast-pocket handkerchief while he waited.

The door was opened by Rose Heminway, an attractive widow in her early thirties. She had shoulder-length blonde hair, and was wearing tapered green slacks and a vest of the same material. Painter suppressed a small gulp. He was seeing her in slacks for the first time, and these particular slacks were very effective, though so tight that he thought she probably had trouble putting them on.

"It didn't take you long to get here, Mr. Painter," she said, smiling. "I've been listening for your siren."

"I don't always use it," Painter said. He followed her in. "And after all the time we've spent together the last few weeks, don't you think we could start using first names?"

She smiled over her shoulder. "A fine idea, Peter. I was going to suggest it myself. But I confess I had an ulterior motive when I asked you to stop in. There's something I want to say to you."

They went into a pleasantly-furnished living room. In daylight the big windows across one end of the room would give a good view of the north bay. She saw him looking at a huge abstract painting on another wall. "Like it?"

"Very much," he said doubtfully.

"It's my pride and joy. Sit down, Peter. I think you'll find the sofa most comfortable."

He sat where she pointed, being careful with the creases in his pants. "Now don't tell me we have to go into the Sam Harris case any more. I was afraid you'd bring it up, but haven't we exhausted that subject? I know it's exhausted me."

She leaned over a tray on the low table in front of the sofa and put ice in a highball glass. "Norma Harris came to see me again this afternoon. Scotch or bourbon?"

"Bourbon, thanks. And what did dear, sweet Norma have to say? It couldn't be anything new. I must have heard her repertoire of insults fifty times by now."

She made the drinks and handed him his, then sat down at the opposite end of the sofa, bringing up her knees between them.

"She's getting frantic, Peter. Really and truly frantic. I thought she was on the point of screaming a few times, and I don't know that I blame her. The execution's only five days away. She says that when she went to your office today you refused to see her."

Painter flicked impatiently at his little hairline mustache. "There's no reason I should waste my time on every kooky dame who keeps coming in and having hysterics and turning the place into a madhouse. How do you think we can get any work done with that going on? We have other problems besides hers."

"I understand that, Peter, but I can understand her position, too. Time's running short."

"I'm aware of that," Painter said. "There's a big red ring around the date on my calendar. I don't need to be reminded of it every hour on the hour. In my humble opinion, she's putting on the loyal wife act a little late. The woman's no better than a chippy. I may be doing her an injustice, but I don't really think so."

He tasted the highball and shook it to make the ice-cubes rattle. "What else did she say to you? You sounded—I don't know how to describe it, sort of strained on the phone."

"Did I?" she said. "I probably did. Whenever I'm talking to somebody who feels that strongly about something, they can always manage to convince me. It's only when I brood about it afterward that I begin to have doubts. Well, I might as well tell you. She—she says she's sure you've turned up some new evidence which you're deliberately suppressing. Don't say anything for a minute, Peter. I know it's ridiculous. I know you wouldn't be a party to anything like that. But I can see how her mind works.

"You handled the original case against her husband. She's given you some new leads, and it really hasn't seemed to me that you've been—well, too energetic about following them up. You're the expert, and there's probably a perfectly good reason. I don't think you'd deliberately sit on something, just to protect yourself against a charge of being stupid or careless three years ago. That's what Mrs. Harris thinks, however, and she's working herself up to giving it to the papers. She's still quite a good looking girl. They might make quite a big thing out of it."

"I don't think I'll worry about that," Painter said calmly, drinking.

She hesitated. "There's one other thing. As I say, she can be very persuasive. It's her idea to call a press conference in her lawyer's office, and she wants me to be there to back her up. She's right about one thing—it would be an effective piece of publicity. Her husband was sentenced to death for killing mine. If she tells the newspapers she thinks he's innocent, that's not such a sensational piece of news. But if I say the same—"

Painter's eyes narrowed. "Do you mean to sit there and tell me you intend to associate yourself publicly with this psycopath? You're going to accuse me of letting an innocent man go to his death, for fear of being blamed for a shoddy piece of police work three years ago?"

She refused to meet his eyes. "I wouldn't put it exactly that way, Peter. But it *has* been almost three weeks since I came to you, and as far as I can see you haven't accomplished a blessed thing."

He stirred uneasily. "I keep telling you I'm working on it."

"I accepted that at first, but it's just too vague, Peter. Never mind Norma. Never mind me. Think about Sam Harris in his condemned cell. Surely that same date is marked in red on his calendar, and every day it comes one day nearer."

Painter half-emptied his glass and balanced it on his knee while he fished for his cigarette-holder and cigarettes. "I have other things to worry about besides how a condemned murderer is passing his time."

She shook her head as he offered her the cigarettes. "But what if he's innocent? What if something turns up six days from now to prove that Norma is right and the jury and everybody else was wrong? It won't help Sam Harris, will it? And I testified against him. How do you think *I'll* feel?"

"I've been in this business a good many years, Rose," Painter said. "Why not accept the fact that I know what I'm doing?"

She shook her head. "I just can't. Norma didn't think we should give you even this long, but I talked her into it. Now she's talked me into doing it her way."

Painter fitted a cigarette into his holder and struck a match. "When are you staging this spectacular press conference?"

"She wanted to call it for tomorrow. I persuaded her to put it off a day, on one condition."

"And what condition is that?" Painter said with a slight smile.

She smoothed the tight green material over her knee. "I can't see why you could possibly object to this, but maybe you'll think I ought to have consulted you first. I'm hiring a private detective."

"You're *what?*"

"And then if he hasn't turned up anything in twenty-four hours, we'll go ahead with the press conference and try to get a stay of execution on the grounds of new evidence. It may not work, but it can't conceivably do any harm. Everybody says that Michael Shayne is the best man we could—"

"Shayne!" Painter cried in horror, and his knee jerked violently. His highball glass flew into the air and came down in his lap.

Rose leaped up. She gathered a handful of small cocktail napkins and thrust them at him. "That drink has been making me nervous. I knew something like that would happen."

He mopped at his pants angrily. "Well, how did I know you were going to mention that bum?"

"I guess I should have asked your advice before I called him," she said. "I take it you know him?"

"I know him, all right," Painter said grimly.

"Give me your glass. I'll make another drink."

"No, never mind." He picked up the spilled ice cubes, put them in his empty glass and set it back on the table. "How far has this gone? Have you paid him any money?"

"Not yet. He hasn't agreed he'll take the case, actually. I have a date to talk to him about it in the morning."

"Good," Painter said with relief. "Then it's not too late to call it off. Take my advice, Rose. Don't waste your money. You might as well drop it in a sewer, for all the good it'll do you. I really have been working, no matter what Norma Harris thinks. Why hire somebody to go over the same ground?"

"But we don't know what you've been doing, don't you see? We can't take it on faith any longer."

"Well, you have to take it on faith."

"Then I'm sorry," she said stubbornly. "I made an agreement with Norma, and I'll have to stick to it."

Painter ran his fingers through his hair. "Go ahead. It's your money. But if you won't be happy unless you hire a private detective, for the love of God stay away from Michael Shayne. I'll give you the name of a good man on the Beach. He has some competent people working for him, and what's more important, he has the cooperation and confidence of the police authorities. Unlike Shayne, he keeps out of the headlines."

"But what do you have against Michael Shayne, Peter?" she said, puzzled. "I checked quite carefully, I thought. All the people I talked to said he's done some amazing things."

"What have I got against—" Painter sputtered. "Oh, he's

done amazing things, all right. Nobody's more amazed at the things he gets away with than I am. He's made himself a career out of cutting corners, out of skating on thin ice, using extra-legal methods and flouting authority, undermining the public's confidence in dedicated, hard-working officials who don't do anything glamorous but simply plug away at their jobs year in, year out, for a coolie's wage, not looking for glory or romance—and the bastard's luck!" Painter exclaimed, almost incoherently. "The bastard's blind, dumb luck is beyond belief! I'm asking you as a special favor—don't go to Shayne. He'll crucify me!"

"Crucify you, Peter? I don't see what you're getting so excited about. He hasn't said he'll do it."

"Don't worry about that," Painter said bitterly. "Thanks to that fool luck of his, he's got enough money so he doesn't have to take on any new cases unless he wants to, but I think I can predict that he'll take this one! When he finds out that I'm involved, he'll jump at it. Don't you see? We've been carrying on a running battle over the years. I don't maintain that this has been entirely Shayne's fault.

"I'll admit that where that son of a bitch is concerned, I have trouble controlling my temper. Excuse the language, Rose, but I can't speak about that big red-headed slob in ordinary English. He hates my guts. I hate his. If he thinks he sees a chance to discredit me, to prove that I'm trying to railroad an innocent man to his death, he won't eat, he won't sleep. Wait and see."

"I'm sure he's intelligent enough to know there's no question of *that*, Peter."

"Maybe. But in this day and age you don't have to prove something if you repeat it often enough. Shayne has some close friends on the papers, and they'll give him all the breaks. I know that man. He'll throw mud at me with both hands, and maybe in the end he'll succeed in convincing a few morons that the police work in the Harris case left something to be desired, and I'm trying to cover it up. Believe me, Rose, if you're thinking about Harris, this is the worst possible thing you can do. Shayne would be so busy trying to build a case against me that he wouldn't have time for anything else."

"But—wouldn't it amount to the same thing, Peter? I'm not trying to be sarcastic—I'd really like to know. If he actually has this terrific hostility against you, wouldn't he try to show that Harris is innocent?"

Painter made a move to stand up. "It's no use talking to you. Sam Harris is no damn good, and that's all there is to it. Neither is his wife, and why a person like you should get so wrought up over that precious couple, I'll never understand. You aren't committed to Shayne. Let me give you this other name."

She frowned. "No, Norma would never agree to that. She was dead set against the whole idea until I happened to mention Michael Shayne. Maybe she's heard about this antipathy between you."

Painter removed his carefully folded handkerchief and patted his mouth. "You're forcing my hand, and I wish you'd have a little confidence in me and let me set my own schedule, but if you won't, you won't. Will you at least do this? Postpone your meeting with Shayne until the afternoon?"

She studied him. "But why?"

"I can't tell you that. But I can promise you one thing. By noon tomorrow the whole question will be academic, and you can save yourself some money. You won't need a private detective."

"I don't know why you have to make such a mystery of this," she said. "But if you think it's that important . . ."

"I do," he assured her, and went to her phone. "And I'd like you to change that appointment right now, if you don't mind, so it won't be weighing on me." He didn't have to look up the number, but dialed it from memory. He held out the phone. "You'll get the switchboard at his hotel. Whatever you do, don't tell him this was my idea. He'd start moving on it right away. Sometimes I swear I think that redhead can see around corners. I don't think you'd even better mention you've been talking to me."

When the hotel clerk answered Rose asked for Mr. Michael Shayne. "Oh?" she said. "Do you know where he can be reached? . . . I see. Will you see that he gets a message? Ask him to call Mrs. Rose Heminway when he comes in, at this number."

She dictated her phone number and gave the phone to Painter, who put it back for her.

"But don't count on that message getting to him. Keep trying." He gave his mustache a quick downward flick, as though to make sure that the hairs were still growing in the right direction. "*Hell!*"

"I'm sorry," she said helplessly. "I honestly didn't expect this to be such a bombshell. At least we've disposed of it now. Won't you change your mind about that drink?"

"Thank you, Rose. But some other night. I couldn't relax. If I'm going to beat Shayne to the punch I'd better step things up a bit."

She got up. "More mystery, Peter. I hope you really know what you're doing."

"Listen to the twelve o'clock news tomorrow," he said smugly.

He started for the door, frowning importantly. Rose had given him a bad moment when she told him about Shayne, but he had hold of himself now. He saw new possibilities, in fact. It would make his triumph that much sweeter. This time, he promised himself, if Shayne tried to stick his nose into something that didn't concern him, the infuriating private detective who had bested Painter so often would end up flat on his back with a surprised look on his big ugly face.

And Painter was also enjoying the way Rose was looking at him, puzzled but at the same time respectful. Women seldom looked at him like that, particularly women as good looking as Rose. He didn't know why this should be so. Somebody had once told him that he would be better off if he could only develop a sense of humor, but just because he happened to believe in taking serious things seriously—

And at that point in his reflections, his heel came down on

an ice cube that had escaped from the drink he had spilled. His leg shot out at a sickening angle, his arms sawed the air, and he landed with a crash. Rose stooped over him with a little cry. She couldn't have been more solicitous and helpful, but Painter thought he could see a faint quirk at the corner of her mouth. She would dissolve in mirth the moment he was gone.

He felt his spine. Nothing seemed to be dislocated, luckily, but he needed help to get to his feet. He mumbled something, feeling his face prickle with embarrassment.

"I'm terribly, terribly sorry," she said. "Are you—"

"Perfectly all right," he said stiffly.

"Don't you think you'd better sit down for a minute?"

"Certainly not."

"Well—"

As Rose opened the front door for him, Heinemann came out from the shadow of a tree and crossed to the Cadillac. Rose watched solicitously until Painter was in the back seat with the door closed.

"Are you all right, Chief?" Heinemann said.

Painter snapped, "What do you mean, am I all right?"

"Nothing, except it looked like you were walking sort of funny."

Painter suppressed a strong impulse to massage the injured spot. "What's holding us up, Heinemann? I want to stop at my apartment. Let's go, damn it! Use the siren."

2

PULLING UP IN front of his apartment building, one of an impressive row on a cross street in the northern section of Miami Beach, Painter grated, "This would be a good time not to fall asleep, Heinemann. I'm in the phone book, and if anybody wants to find out where I live they can look it up."

"I'm wide awake, Chief," Heinemann said.

"Check the foyer."

Heinemann looked inside the vestibule and up and down the sidewalk. He kept one hand on his gun while Painter left the Cadillac and entered the building. Alone in the automatic elevator, Painter allowed himself to slump forward to ease the tension at the base of his spine. He probed the affected area, wincing. Worse than the pain was the recollection of the faint hint of amusement at the corner of Rose Heminway's mouth. But he couldn't really blame her. He hadn't thought it was funny himself, but to an observer it had probably been one of the funniest pratfalls since Buster Keaton was in his prime.

The elevator took him to the eighth floor. Determined not to let the pain slow him down, he walked briskly down the corridor, feeling in his pockets for his keys. He had a lot to do, if he was going to be ready by the time Mike Shayne appeared on the scene. He sorted out his door-key and half-raised it as he came to his door.

He stopped, surprised. The door was slightly ajar. He reached for the doorknob, but checked himself, a wary expression on his face. He listened. He put his keys away, took out his .38 and snapped off the safety. He listened again, then gave the door a quick push and stepped back against the wall.

Nothing happened. All the lights were on in his living room. Moving with great care, he slid around the edge of the door and stopped, appalled. Several drawers of his desk had been pulled out and dumped on the floor. The pillows had been pulled off the sofa and the chairs. Pictures had been yanked from the walls, the carpet had been thrown back. Looking around at this shambles, he felt a slow rage begin to build up inside him.

He went through the door into the bedroom, moving according to the manual, slowly at first, then fast. This room, too, had been visited by the same strong wind. The lock on his three-drawer filing cabinet had been forced, and the drawers had been pulled out. Even now, before he checked to see if the Sam Harris file was missing, his policeman's instinct told him to look into the bathroom and the closets and to be sure that no one was concealed on the fire escape. Only then did he put away his gun and crouch beside the lowermost drawer. He had been swearing savagely under his breath, but now he had stopped. This was beyond the reach of words.

Suddenly there was a low moan behind him.

Painter dove to one side, very fast, and grabbed at the .38. He was in a bad position and the gun stuck in its holster. For an instant he thought it wouldn't come out, and he felt the beginnings of panic. He was trapped! He worried at the harness with his left hand and went on yanking at the gun until it broke free. He was lying on his side near the foot of his bed. There was another moan, more nearly a sigh. Painter inched forward, pushing the gun ahead of him, and saw a man's shoe.

"Don't move!" he said, his voice rising.

He came to one knee. He was wound up tight. The bedding had been thrown off the bed and a man was lying behind the untidy pile, partly hidden by it. Painter straightened carefully, his trigger-finger tense, ready to fire. He went on moving until he could see the man's face.

It was pitted with tiny pockmarks. There was an ugly gash

on one temple, and that whole side of his face was a mass of blood. His eyes were open, but they seemed glazed. Painter had never seen him before.

He kicked the bedclothes aside. He could see both of the man's hands now. One of the hands twitched and he said sharply, "I told you not to move, and that's what I meant."

When he saw that both hands were empty, he went on taking a policeman's precautions, patting the man in the various places where a gun can be carried. Then he returned his .38 to its holster.

He went down into a crouch. "Who are you?" he demanded.

The man breathed in and out with great effort. "Painter?" he whispered.

"What about it?"

"I'm—Gray. McNarney Committee."

His voice was so faint that Painter was barely able to catch the words. He rocked back on his heels. The McNarney Committee! At the moment the McNarney Committee was making headlines with an investigation of labor racketeering, but how in God's name had they got wind of this? Apparently they could smell a front-page story all the way from Washington, D. C. Now Painter really had to hurry, or it would get away from him. He knew his limitations. He couldn't compete with a standing committee of the United States Senate, with its access to the newspapers, unlimited funds, its staff of investigators and lawyers.

"Who slugged you?" he said hoarsely.

The man gestured with one hand. "Big. Rugged. Red hair."

"A *redhead?*" Painter exclaimed.

Gray made a small hurt sound. He touched his temple, then looked at the blood on his fingers. He moaned again and tried to come to his elbows, but the effort was too much for him and he fell back.

Painter gripped his shirtfront with both hands.

"Now take your time," he said urgently. "Tell me what happened."

Gray gathered himself to speak. "Door open."

"Yes?" Painter said impatiently when the injured man stopped to breathe heavily. "The door was open. Somebody was inside?"

Gray gave an almost inperceptible nod. "Went in. Dumb, no gun. Man—behind door. Just one punch. Like kick of a mule. Fell. Hit my head."

"Now listen to me," Painter said, tightening his grip. "I'll get you an ambulance in a minute, but before I go off half-cocked I have to be a hundred percent sure. Was this guy six feet and a couple of inches, big shoulders—" He stopped. He had a vivid picture of Mike Shayne in his mind's eye—he probably thought about the rangy private detective more than was good for his mental health—but describing him in a hurry was a hard thing to do. "Solid, all bone and muscle. Deep lines on his face. There's a little gray in that red hair now. I don't know, damn it—he's the kind of man the girls go for, for some strange reason."

The man on the floor nodded, and the nod turned into a tremor that he couldn't control. "Who is he?"

"Who is he?" Painter cried triumphantly. "That's Michael Shayne, man, and this is one time he's going to wish he'd never tangled with me. Don't die, please, Gray. Get well. I'm going to need your testimony." He gave a happy little chortle. "When I'm done with the son of a bitch, he'll be selling live bait to the tourists in Bay Front Park."

He seized the phone and began to dial, but in his excitement his finger slipped and he had to start over. This time he did it right, and in a moment he was connected with Beach headquarters.

"Painter," he snapped. "I'm at home. I want Joe Wing and two men up here right away. And get out a pick-up call on Mike Shayne to all cars."

"Who, Chief?" the sergeant asked. "*Shayne?*"

"What do you want me to do, spell it for you? Breaking and entering, and assault with intent to kill. I don't want them to park outside his hotel and hope he'll show up. I want them to look for him. He drives a black Buick. License number—" He thought for a moment and dictated a number, which was another of the numerous facts about Shayne that he kept in his head, in the hope that sometime they would prove useful. "I don't want a single car to stay in the garage. Put it strong when you tell the boys across the Bay, because those bastards have been known to get forgetful all of a sudden where Mike Shayne is concerned."

"Ambulance," Gray said weakly.

"Yeah, and I want an ambulance," Painter said.

Suddenly he heard a heavy hammering noise from the street below. He exclaimed, *"Was that a shot?"*

Gray's head had lifted. Painter thrust his hand inside his coat. Before either of them could speak, there were two more sharp pistol shots and Painter threw the phone back on its cradle. Gray tried to fight forward, but he fell back and his eyes closed.

"Shayne?" he whispered.

"We'll find out," Painter said grimly, drawing his gun.

He ran into the other room, hearing Gray call weakly, "Good—hunting."

He sprinted to the elevator. As always happened when he wanted it in a hurry, it was being used by somebody else. He kept his thumb on the button, hearing the soft, patient whir of the machinery. It rose to the top floor, stayed there for what seemed to Painter an incredibly long time, and started down at last, moving slowly and unhurriedly.

When it finally arrived, one of his fellow-tenants was inside, an elderly maiden lady who gasped excitedly when she saw the bared gun.

"Mr. Painter! Is anything wrong?"

"Possible, madam," he snarled. "Very possible."

The elevator resumed its calm descent. She wet her lips.

"Perhaps you'd better let me off?"

He exclaimed in annoyance, and his hand started toward the control panel. She said quickly, "No, on second thoughts. I wouldn't ever forgive myself. Certain people I could mention are going to have a fit when I tell them about it. Who are you after, if I may ask?"

"That's neither here nor there," Painter said gruffly. "Stand back, please. And don't leave the elevator under any circumstances."

"Goodness!"

The door opened. As Painter burst out into the lobby he crashed into an old man who was waiting. He untangled himself with difficulty. The old lady called out, "He's chasing somebody, Henry! Did you ever expect a thing like that to happen right here in the Royal Palms?"

"He's being damned clumsy about it, I must say," the old man said.

Painter ran out to the street. Heinemann was nowhere in sight.

"Heinemann!" Painter yelled.

He was answered by another quick shot, coming from the direction of Collins Avenue. He dashed toward the corner, but checked himself abruptly and was careful going around it. He ducked into a store entrance.

This was usually a busy part of town, but there was nothing moving on the sidewalk now but a solitary cat. Several people cowered behind benches on the surfside. On the road itself the usual night-time traffic continued to roll. Painter was about to leave his shelter when a tall, hatless figure ran toward a parked car with a gun in his hand. As he passed beneath a street light Painter saw the set of the broad shoulders and the red hair. Nobody, he thought, but Mike Shayne had shoulders like that, combined with hair that particular shade.

Painter darted after him, but he realized almost at once that he couldn't make it. His quarry jumped into the car. The motor came to life. It was a black Buick, and as it shot away from the curb, Painter saw the familiar license number. He levelled his gun, aiming at a tire. But before he could fire the Buick slid smoothly into the line of traffic. Painter swore and raced back around the corner toward his unattended Cadillac.

"Heinemann!" he shouted again. "Goddam it, *where the hell are you?*"

There was no answer. As he ran, he sorted out the duplicate ignition key from the others in his pocket. Giving one last frantic look around for his driver, he leaped in and fumbled the key into the ignition. The powerful motor responded with a full-throated roar. Painter wrenched at the wheel, hitting the gas hard. He touched the knob controlling the siren, but didn't activate it. Not yet. If Shayne was held up at the next red light, Painter might be able to get on his tail and find out where he was going. If not, using the siren and the blinkers, he would run him off the road.

He turned the corner on the outside of his tires, leaving a smear behind him on the pavement. A line of cars was waiting for the light. For a moment he thought the Buick wasn't among them. He closed the gap very fast, and by edging over the double line down the middle of the street he saw the car he wanted, first in line.

Painter chuckled to himself, leaning tensely over the wheel. Shayne had got away with some pretty tricky operations over the years, many of them at Painter's expense. But not this time, Painter promised himself. Not this time. He was going to make the big redhead wish he had taken up some different line of work, and had never had the bad luck to run afoul of Chief-of-Detectives Peter Painter.

3

A FEW MINUTES AFTER five the next morning, Michael Shayne wheeled his Buick into a parking slot near his apartment hotel on the north bank of the Miami River. He looked at his watch and gave a relaxed snort of laughter. Five a.m. This had been a night!

He switched off his lights, noticing that he hadn't really needed the full beam for the last ten minutes. The sun was about due. He took the key out of the ignition and cranked up the windows. As he stepped out onto the street, slamming the door, a thin young man moved up against him swiftly and hit him in the lower ribs with the muzzle of a pistol.

"Stand still!" he said almost eagerly.

Shayne froze, his hands out in the dim light. From that position he could chop upward with his elbow at his assailant's throat, but he could feel the young man's tension, and he did what he had been ordered to do: he held still.

Another man appeared around the front of the car. Shayne knew this one.

"Joe Wing," he said, and let himself relax slightly. "It's nice to see a familiar face. I thought this was a stick-up."

"Don't say anything, Mike," Wing said.

He was a lean lieutenant with a nervous manner and an emaciated-looking face, a good cop who in Shayne's opinion deserved a better fate than having to work under Peter Painter. He went over Shayne carefully for weapons.

"What's the theory, Joe?" Shayne said. "I've gone to work for the Mafia?"

Joe Wing stepped back. "When I said not to say anything, that's what I meant. I want you to answer some questions. I don't want you to ask any. Where have you been all night?"

Shayne lowered his big hands. "Around," he said. "But I'm not very good at answering questions when somebody's pointing a gun at me. It makes me restless."

After a moment's thought Wing nodded, and the gun went back in its holster. "Now I'll say it again," he said. "Where have you been all night?"

"Playing poker," Shayne told him.

"Playing poker," Wing repeated. "That's a nice sociable activity. When did the game get underway?"

"Come on, now," Shayne said brusquely. "You've been working out of Painter's office so long you're beginning to sound like him. You've got the look of a man who's been awake all night. I've been on all-night stakeouts myself, and I know they don't improve the disposition. But it doesn't improve mine to have a gun shoved in my ribs, either, especially when it's a rookie who's doing the shoving, and he's a little tense. If the police department's in trouble I'll be glad to cooperate, but I'd like to be asked politely. Take me in, if that's the way you want to handle it. You might be able to hold me as long as twenty-four hours, if you're lucky, and you can ask a lot of questions in that time. I doubt if you'd get any answers. That's one way. The other way is to come upstairs and have a drink and start fresh."

Wing pushed his hat off his forehead. He stared at Shayne for a long moment.

"All right, Mike," he said wearily. "I could argue about it, but we'd probably end up doing it your way, as usual. I want those answers, and if the only way I can get them is by sitting down in a comfortable chair and drinking your liquor, I guess I'll just have to force myself. Call in, Thompson," he told the other detective. "The big manhunt is over. Tell them to locate Heinemann and have him report here."

then I picked up a pizza at a joint near the airport. How much detail do you want on this?"

"Just the highspots for now. You were alone at that point?"

"Yeah."

Shayne rubbed the day-old stubble on his chin, remembering. He had not only been alone, he had been the only solitary eater in the crowded restaurant. He had been painfully aware of the fact. The truth was, he had come to depend on Lucy Hamilton's company at the end of the day more than he liked to admit.

He continued: "The place was jammed, and I must have been there—oh, maybe an hour. I was in no rush. I went back to the airport bar and had a few more drinks. Then I decided to kill some time at the movies."

"What movie?" Wing said quickly.

"It turned out there wasn't anything I wanted to see. I came in to the Beach and hit a few bars. When I ran into Tim Rourke it must have been around ten. Maybe nine-thirty, maybe ten-thirty, and it won't do you any good to ask Tim, because that late at night he doesn't keep track of the time. He wanted to play some poker. We rounded up a few people and went to his place. You'll be happy to hear that I was the big winner."

Wing looked anything but happy. He was scribbling in a notebook. "Who were the other players besides you and Rourke?"

Shayne told him.

"Even Petey wouldn't make you boys put in all this overtime without a good reason," Shayne said. "Give me a specific time. Maybe I can be more definite."

Wing didn't look up. "Let's say between eight-thirty and nine."

Shayne frowned. "I'd say that would be about when I was in a place called the Three Deuces on the Beach, near Washington and Fifth. I haven't given them any business in a long time. One of the bartenders used to be a good friend of mine. Gus Pappas. He might remember when I came in, but there was a good crowd there and I was moving around. I don't think anybody would want to swear to the whole half hour. I wouldn't swear to it myself."

Wing and LaBanca exchanged a look. Wing said, "What kind of transportation were you using, Mike? Your own car, or taxi?"

"I had the Buick. I'd like a little information, Joe. Is somebody dead?"

"People are dying all the time. When was the last time you saw Painter?"

"That's something else that happens pretty often," Shayne said. "I hear a siren, and there he is. That man is getting siren-happy."

"Wing started to smile, but he quickly suppressed it. "That's not what I mean, as you probably know. Have you had any business with him lately?"

"I haven't had any business with anybody lately. I've been turning people away, or Miss Hamilton has been turning them away for me. I got pretty well knocked around on that last case, not that I was the only one. She's been trying to get me to take a rest."

"Well, there's a definite statement, finally," Wing said. "Do I understand you to say that you aren't working on anything at the moment?"

"That's right," Shayne said easily. "Write it down."

"What about this Mrs. Heminway who's been calling you?"

"I'm supposed to see her in the morning." He looked at his watch. "And unless you boys let me get some sleep, I'm not going to be very goddam bright-eyed. It's your turn now, Joe. What happened last night between eight-thirty and nine?"

"You really don't know, Mike?" Wing said softly.

He took his notebook to Shayne's phone, and rattled until he woke up the clerk downstairs. He asked to speak with the detective in the lobby. When the man came on he relayed the names Shayne had just given him, and told him to find out if they'd run into Mike Shayne recently.

"They won't like that," Shayne said. "They just got to bed about fifteen minutes ago."

Wing said into the phone, "Has Heinemann come in yet? . . . Send him up to Shayne's room. Now tell the clerk to give me an outside line, and keep the switch open so you can make notes on the call." He looked around at Shayne. "I'm going to dial Mrs. Heminway's number for you now, Mike, if you don't mind."

"Hell, yes, I mind," Shayne said. "But I know that's not going to cut any ice with you."

When Wing had a dialtone he looked up a number in the book beneath the table. "She said to call her when you came in. She didn't say not to call her if you didn't get in till five in the morning."

Shayne finished the cognac without hurrying. After dialing the number Wing handed him the phone. It rang several times, and a woman's voice said sleepily, "Yes?"

"This is Michael Shayne," the redhead said. "I've got some cops here, and they thought I ought to call you. It wasn't my idea. Go back to sleep, and I'll call again at a civilized hour."

"Oh, Mr. Shayne," she said. "No. Wait a minute till I pull myself together. Did you say something about—cops?"

Shayne grinned across at Joe Wing. "The whole Beach detective force has been looking for me all night, it seems. I don't know if that means anything to you. If it does we'd better talk about it later. When was our appointment? Nine?"

"Yes. But wait, Mr. Shayne. That's what I wanted to tell you. My wits are all over the place. Mr. Painter wants me to put that off till afternoon. Could you make it at one instead?" She gave an exclamation of dismay. "I wasn't supposed to tell you that Mr. Painter asked me."

"One o'clock's fine, Mrs. Heminway," Shayne said quickly. "Maybe they'll let me get some sleep before then."

He broke the connection. Wing took the phone and asked the detective in the lobby for Mrs. Heminway's end of the conversation. He hung up sadly.

"You haven't really started cooperating yet, have you, Mike?"

"I've had a few arguments with your boss on that point," Shayne said bleakly. "If my clients want the cops to know about their problem, they don't bring it to me. On top of that, I don't like to have people listening in on my phone conversations."

There was a respectful tap on the door. Wing let in another detective Shayne had seen around Beach headquarters. He wore a strong look of resentment, as though he had a grievance against society, and an X of adhesive tape over a shaved place at the back of his head.

"Take a good look at him, Heinemann," Wing said.

Heinemann stared at Shayne suspiciously, then walked around him in a half-circle. Shayne turned.

"Do you want both profiles, or just one?"

"He's got the build," Heinemann said doubtfully. "And the hair. But if you want to know if I can pick him out of a show-up, Lieutenant, let's say I'd like to think it over some more."

"That adhesive tape on your skull hasn't had time to get dirty yet," Shayne said. "When did you get slugged, between eight-thirty and nine?"

"About ten of nine," Heinemann said, "give or take a couple of minutes."

Joe Wing said sharply, "That's enough of that. And if you don't have the sense to keep your mouth shut, we may have to decorate you with more adhesive tape, in a new place."

"All I said was—" But he wilted under the lieutenant's look, and didn't go on.

Wing helped himself to more Scotch. "I'll ask you again, Mike, and this time I'll leave off the please. Why does Mrs. Heminway want to hire you? And if you don't feel like answering, we'll get the State's Attorney to repeat the question in front of a jury."

Shayne made a rude noise. "That's Petey's speech, Joe, and I'm surprised to hear it from you. The legal ground is very shaky. You can't get me up before a grand jury in less than three days, and that's the minimum. You wouldn't have been waiting for me all night unless you were in a hurry."

"Goddam it, Mike, one of these days—"

"That's Painter's speech, too," Shayne said, breaking in. "And now that we're on that unpleasant subject, where *is* Painter? How come he's letting you ask the questions?"

Wing looked at him narrowly. The phone rang and Wing picked it up. He listened for a moment.

"Did you contact the bartender?" There was another pause, and he said, "Keep trying Rourke. Get a key from his superintendent and pull him out of bed if you have to."

Hanging up, he turned back to Shayne. "The poker game story seems to check, and for your sake I hope those witnesses haven't had any coaching. Pappas, the bartender, thinks you made the Three Deuces around eight, but he didn't have you under observation every minute you were there. He gave us some leads, which we can't check out till tonight. You could save us some trouble, you know, Mike. Isn't it a fact that you left the Three Deuces sometime around eight-thirty and drove to Painter's apartment house at the other end of the Beach?"

Shayne's eyes glittered. He uncorked the cognac bottle and refilled his glass. "Why would I do a thing like that?" he said gently.

"That's what I'd like to have you tell us. It has to be connected in some way with these calls you've been getting from Mrs. Heminway. And don't give me one of those know-nothing looks. Painter left her house shortly after eight and went home to pick up something at his apartment. Heinemann was driving him. Mrs. Heminway says he asked her to postpone seeing you. What is all this, just a coincidence?"

"I don't go out of my way to see Petey," Shayne said, drinking. "I see him often enough as it is. Now what about these searching looks I keep getting from Heinemann?"

Wing hesitated. "All right, and God knows if I'm doing the right thing. You could be milking me, to find out how much we know. A few minutes after Painter went upstaris, Heinemann heard a gun go off down the block. He went to see who was shooting. As he went around the corner he got a quick glimpse of somebody running across the street with a gun in his hand. You've just heard him say that this person was your size and build, with red hair. Then he was rapped from behind. He woke up with a bad headache. He was lying in the foyer of one of the apartment buildings, tied up and gagged. An old dame from Painter's building found him."

Shayne rolled the cognac around in his mouth and swallowed it, following it with a sip of ice water. "That's pretty flimsy, Joe. Heinemann caught a fast glimpse of somebody who looked vaguely like me, and you mobilized the whole force and stayed up all night. What's so important it can't wait till morning? If you're going to tell me, don't dole it out a crumb at a time."

The room was quiet while Wing made up his mind.

"If that's how you want it, Mike. I don't like to do it this way, because I've seen Painter try it and it never worked with him. I'll give you one last chance. Cooperate, starting now, or we take you in and book you for resisting arrest."

"I haven't resisted arrest."

"You will, Mike. You will." The ice cubes were making too much noise in his glass, and he put it on the table. "We can hold you longer than twenty-four hours if we work at it. I don't know how long will bother you. You'll miss your appointment with Mrs. Heminway, for one thing. We'll be working while you twiddle your thumbs. You tend to stick out of a crowd, Mike. Maybe somebody else saw you in Painter's neighborhood at ten minutes to nine."

Shayne felt absently for a cigarette. "Somebody finally shot the little Napoleon?"

"It's no laughing matter," Wing said.

"I'm not laughing." Shayne's lighter flared. "But I'm not crying, either."

Wing leaned forward, his fingers tightly laced. "*Where is he, Mike?*"

"How should I know?" Shayne said irritably. "Nobody appointed me Painter's guardian, and if they did I'd refuse the appointment. You know how I feel about the little bastard. But it's finally beginning to dawn on me that Painter's missing. Who saw him last?"

Wing answered reluctantly, "The same old lady who found Heinemann. They came down in the elevator together and he had his gun out. She saw him drive off very fast in his Cad."

"That bus sticks out of a crowd as much as I do," Shayne said. "Even when he's not playing the siren. Use some of the orthodox police methods Petey's always talking about. You ought to be able to find it."

"We've found it," Wing said heavily. "We found it on a secondary road off Route 9 about fifteen miles north of the city. But Painter wasn't in it."

4

SHAYNE SMILED GRIMLY. "You have my sympathy, boys. I'm all broken up. How are you going to get along without him?"

"Mike—" Wing said dangerously.

Shayne held up his hand. "All right, let's call it a tragedy, and I'll try to take it seriously. But I'm not too surprised. He isn't the most popular man in town. And there's one orthodox police method he doesn't use—he keeps things secret from his own staff. Sooner or later that's bound to lead to trouble. Is this all you're going to tell me?"

Wing started to drink, but put the glass down. "At about twelve minutes to nine, a call came into headquarters. It was Painter, sounding very hopped up and happy. He wanted an ambulance, he wanted me, and he wanted a general pick-up call on Michael Shayne. He told the duty sergeant to cover the causeways and the main exits from town. He said something jumbled about breaking and entering, and assault. The sergeant didn't get all of it. But one thing he did get—Painter wanted you, Mike, and I wouldn't say that all he wanted was to find out if you had anything good in the Daily Double at Hialeah."

Shayne rubbed the reddish stubble along his jaw. "Who was the ambulance for—Heinemann?"

"No, the sequence is wrong. Painter heard the shots while he was talking to headquarters. He seemed to be in his usual health when the old lady saw him a minute or so later, so he didn't want the ambulance for himself. God knows *who* he wanted it for. Unless we're completely off on the timing, he made the call from his apartment. I got the super to open it up. There was no indication that anybody had been there who was sick or hurt."

"Funny," Shayne said thoughtfully.

"And there's something else that's funnier. You know how neat the bast—Painter is. It's a pathological thing with him. The place was presentable enough when I saw it, a lot neater than the way most of us live, but—well, for one thing, the books on the shelves weren't lined up the way they usually are. When Painter sees a book a little out of line, he can't sit still until he dresses it up. There were other things. He subscribes to a couple of magazines—*Time, Reader's Digest,* and he always has them laid out on the coffee table just so, in chronological order. And you can stop grinning, Mike. We all have our quirks."

"Some have more than others," Shayne said.

"I don't deny it. The layout was neat enough, but the dates were all higgeldy-piggeldy, October before June and so on. I'm wondering if he had a fight with somebody."

"This would be a fight that Painter won," Shayne said skeptically.

"That's prejudice," Wing snapped. "Maybe he caught somebody going through his apartment. He carried a gun. Maybe he sapped the intruder to make him hold still while he ran downstairs to find out about the shots. While he was gone, the man came to and straightened the room before he left. Don't ask me why. If you have any better explanation to offer, I'm all ears."

"Don't look at me," Shayne said. "I can't explain anything."

"You can't or you won't?"

Shayne smiled. "It amounts to the same thing, doesn't it, Joe? You've told me a few secrets, and now you expect me to tell you a few in return. But it doesn't work out that way. Petey Painter has always been a mystery to me. Some of the time he seems fairly bright. Some of the time he seems to have an IQ of minus fifty. He's a pain in the behind all the time, but I don't need to tell you that. Logic? I gave up expecting that from Petey long ago."

"Why did Painter want you picked up? Why did he tell your client to put off your appointment? You're in this up to your eyebrows, Mike, and I want to know how."

Shayne's head filled with a sudden pounding, but he forced himself to speak quietly. "Mrs. Heminway's not my client yet, but never mind that. I've had two conversations with her, both on the phone, both brief. You listened in on one of them. All she wanted to know in the other was whether I was available, and on what terms. I'd been wondering what I'd do while Miss Hamilton is out of town, so I said I was available, and the terms would depend on what she wanted me to do. That's all. But I didn't just arrive in Miami from outer space. I read the papers. I know that this Sam Harris who's going to the chair next week killed a minor bank official named Heminway in a robbery.

"I had Tim Rourke dig the stories out of the *News* morgue. Rose Heminway is the dead man's widow. Harris went up on the strength of a bad reputation and two eye-witnesses, one of whom was this same Mrs. Heminway. Petey Painter made the case against him. This all probably means something. I could guess, but I like to let the cops do their own guessing. You won't mind if I shave before I go, will you?"

"Go where?"

"I thought you said you're arresting me."

"Mike, don't be like that. And I thought for a minute you were going to break down and be human, for a change."

The lines around the redhead's mouth deepened. He took his cognac to the bathroom and set it on the glass shelf over the washbowl. From the doorway Joe Wing watched him break out his shaving equipment.

"I'm open to any reasonable compromise," Wing said after a moment. "I know that complete cooperation is probably too much to expect—your quarrel with Painter goes too deep. You can make your own terms."

Shayne went on lathering his face without replying. When

this operation was complete he began stropping his straight razor. Wing stepped into the bathroom and shut the door.

"I wouldn't want to be quoted on this," Wing said in a lower voice, "but I think I share your feelings about Painter, Mike. You see him when you happen to be working on the same case, and that's really not too often. But think of me. I've got him day in and day out. Thank God I'm a patient man. I never used to be, but it's something I've had to develop. As far as I know you're the one man in town with courage enough to tell him off, and listening to you do it is one of my few pleasures in life. That probably goes for most of the men in the department. But that doesn't mean we want to see him killed."

"Keep it in proportion, Joe," Shayne said, beginning to scrape off the lather. "What makes you think anybody killed him? If I have the order right, he was seen driving off after the shots were fired. Did you find any blood in the Cadillac?"

"No," Wing admitted.

"Then there must be something else you haven't told me. How did he happen to be using a driver at that time of night? Especially a plainclothesman like Heinemann. He sounds more like a bodyguard than a driver."

Wing exploded. "Now there's one more fact I've given you, and you still haven't given me one goddam thing. Yeah, he had a twenty-four-hour guard. He was looking forward to fireworks, and he told Heinemann they were up against professionals, or words to that effect. Heinemann can't remember exactly how he put it."

"Do you think I shot him?" Shayne said.

"I didn't say you shot him! But you know more about it than you've told me, and don't deny that again because it's getting monotonous."

Shayne continued shaving methodically, while Wing watched his reflection in the mirror. "If you want something to occupy your mind, here's a point. Harris or whoever hit the Beach Trust three years ago carried away three hundred thousand in cash and bearer bonds. When he was arrested, they found twenty-three thousand under the lining of a suitcase. I think the difference would amount to two hundred and seventy-seven thousand, and where is it?"

"Well?"

"I'm still not getting across to you, Joe. I got those figures out of the *News* clippings, and the only reason I bothered Rourke for them was so I'd have a little background when I talked to Mrs. Heminway. How long has Painter been going around with a bodyguard?"

"Two and a half weeks," Wing said.

"What happened two and a half weeks ago?"

"As far as I know, nothing. The same thing occurred to me, and I've been checking. Nobody remembers anything unusual. He just said he was going to need twenty-four-hour protection until further notice."

"It's a funny way to do business," Shayne commented, working on his lower lip.

"Well it's always been Painter's way," Wing said. "If he pulls something off it's a surprise to everybody, and we stand around and admire him. If it doesn't work we don't know about it. This time I guess it didn't work. Of course if he's turned up by now he won't be glad to hear that I've been dickering with you, Mike. But the Cadillac was abandoned out in the middle of nowhere, with the key still in it. Add that to the shooting, and it worries me. Maybe somebody fired those shots to decoy Heinemann around the corner. The only reason they'd do that would be so they could grab the Chief. You're in the same business we are, in a way. It seems to me you ought to—why the grin, Mike? Did I say anything funny?"

Shayne was grinning broadly. He rinsed off the remains of the lather, and the grin turned into a laugh.

Wing watched him stonily. "Let me in on it, Mike."

Shayne went off into a shout of laughter. He groped blindly for a towel and began to dry his face. Heinemann knocked on the door. "Everything all right in there, Lieutenant?"

"Yeah," Wing growled. "Have a drink. We're leaving in a minute."

"Hell, Joe," Shayne said when he could stop laughing. "Think about it. Whatever this jam turns out to be, he got himself into it by acting even more like Peter Painter than usual. *What if I'm the one who gets him out of it?* It'll damn near kill him."

A smile flickered across Wing's face. "He won't enjoy it. Then you're going to put your cards on the table, Mike?"

"Maybe I don't have any cards to put on the table. That's a possibility, Joe, and this whole thing is weird enough so you shouldn't toss out any possibility. If you want me to make you an offer, here it is. I'll ask Mrs. Heminway what she has in mind, and if I take the case I'll pass on anything I find out, maybe not the minute it comes in, but within a reasonable time."

"That's what I call a hell of a deal."

"It's the only one I can give you, Joe. You might gain something by it. Stick me in jail and all you'll get will be trouble."

"I've got trouble enough now," Wing said, scratching his chin.

"Did Painter see Mrs. Heminway before last night?"

"She came into headquarters two or three times. He didn't take any notes on the visits, and I couldn't find anything with her name on it in the current file."

"Doesn't Painter keep a file of his own at home?"

Wing went on scratching his chin. Then he went to the door and pulled it open abruptly. The two other detectives were helping themselves to Shayne's Scotch.

Heinemann looked up. "Lieutenant?"

"As you were," Wing said, and closed the door. "I hope you don't have this bathroom bugged, Mike, because I'd hate like hell to have Painter find out I'm taking this kind of a handout, and glad to get it. I went through that private file of his, and that's something else I hope nobody ever mentions to him. He uses his own filing system, and it's possible I missed something. I thought of the Sam Harris connection when I heard the name Heminway, but there was nothing in the file under his name or hers, nothing that referred to that old killing in any way."

Shayne said carelessly, "Maybe somebody beat you to the file."

Wing's eyes were narrow and hard. "Maybe. And I hope it wasn't you, Mike."

5

MICHAEL SHAYNE DIALED Mrs. Heminway's number again. Joe Wing was standing close enough to the phone so he could hear both ends of the conversation. This time it rang only twice and the voice that answered was both sleepy and irritated.

"Hello? Who is it?"

"Michael Shayne again, Mrs. Heminway. I hate to do this to you. I know you were probably just getting back to sleep. If I came over in half or three quarters of an hour, could you see me?"

"Good heavens, no," Mrs. Heminway said. "I'm anything but an early riser. As far as I'm concerned this is still the middle of the night. Why the urgency, Mr. Shayne? Only a few minutes ago you were saying—"

"I know. But things have changed. I'd like to get going on it right away."

"Now wait a minute. Has Mr. Peter Painter been throwing his weight around, by any chance?"

Shayne looked at Lieutenant Wing. His shaggy eyebrows rose. "No, I haven't seen Petey for a couple of weeks. What makes you ask that?"

"Oh—you said something about detectives, and it occurred to me that Mr. Painter might have been rash enough to try to put pressure on you directly. I understand you two aren't on very good terms, I mean personally."

"That's a fair statement," Shayne said, grinning. "Personally and every other way. No, these were Petey's boys, but he wasn't with them. Put pressure on me to do what?"

"Not to take the case. I don't think I've ever seen a man as upset as he was when I told him I was planning to hire you. But I made that promise in good faith, and I'm afraid I'll have to stick to it, Mr. Shayne. One o'clock, then?"

"Mrs. Heminway, did you run into a Lieutenant Wing when you went to see Painter?"

"I believe I did. But—"

"I'm putting him on the line."

He handed the phone to Wing, who said, "Joe Wing speaking. Mrs. Heminway, you'll be doing us a favor if you'll talk to Shayne now instead of waiting. The Chief isn't here now, but he wouldn't want to hold you to that promise."

"He certainly wanted to hold me to it last night. Well, you've succeeded in arousing my curiosity, if that was what you were trying to do. Tell Mr. Shayne I'll want a full explanation. Half an hour?"

Wing hung up. "What do you make of that, Mike?"

"What do *I* make of it? What do you make of it? Did he have anything on his calendar for this morning?"

"Nothing but routine."

"Nothing but routine!" Shayne said angrily. "Didn't he have anybody he could trust?"

"Not in the police department, I guess. Mike—" He broke off. "LaBanca. Heinemann. Go on downstairs. I'll be with you in a minute."

"Won't you need some help, Lieutenant?" Heinemann said, looking at the redhead.

"No, I won't need any help!" Wing snapped. "We're not arresting Shayne after all."

"He talked his way out of it, did he?" Heinemann said.

Wing made a threatening gesture. When the two detectives were out of the room he turned to Shayne.

"I still don't know if I'm doing the right thing, but maybe we'll get a little extra this way. Just don't try to play it too cute with me, Mike, because if you do—"

"I'll live to regret it," Shayne said impatiently. "Save your breath, Joe. I've heard it from Painter."

"I happen to mean it," Wing said.

"And while we're laying down the ground rules," Shayne went on, "don't put a tail on me. That's what Petey would do in this situation, but if I spot anybody behind me our deal is off and it's every man for himself."

"Sure, sure," Wing said. "Now we don't want to keep the lady waiting."

Shayne finished knotting his tie. He poured a last shot of cognac. Then he found a fresh package of cigarettes and they went out.

The Bay Harbor Islands are several small man-made keys in upper Biscayne Bay, joined by the Broad Causeway. Michael Shayne parked on the white clamshell driveway beside Mrs. Heminway's handsome house. The grounds were carefully landscaped and they seemed to be well looked after. As he crunched along the shell path to the front door, he noted the boathouse and dock, the smooth putting-green lawn, the flowering shrubs, and he put a price-tag of $65,000 on the property.

Rose Heminway opened the door for him. Shayne saw a good-looking athletic woman with blonde hair, widely spaced blue eyes and a pleasant mouth. She was wearing a dark-red belted wrapper and high-heeled slippers. Shayne had given her ample time to put on make-up and brush her hair, and she had done both.

She looked at him with approval. "You couldn't be anybody else but Mr. Michael Shayne. I've heard you described. Come in. I think the coffee's done."

She took him all the way through to a large kitchen, filled with the agreeable smell of freshly-percolated coffee. "You'll have a cup, Mr. Shayne?"

"Mmm," he said. "Yes, thanks."

"That doesn't sound too enthusiastic." She looked over her shoulder. "I was a little fuzzy when I talked to you on the phone. I took a pill to get to sleep, and I'm afraid I didn't make much sense. Did I gather that you haven't been to bed yet? Maybe you'd rather have a drink. Or some brandy in your coffee?"

Shayne grinned. "The service seems to be very good around here."

"Sit down, Mr. Shayne. I don't often see this room at this time of morning. It's actually quite pleasant, isn't it?"

She waved at an alcove which was getting the early sun. She clicked from the refrigerator to the stove, to a counter, back to the refrigerator and then across to the table with a tray. He was satisfied to sit and watch. She moved well, and the robe moved in interesting ways of its own, opening and closing. She produced a bottle of brandy and poured a large slug in Shayne's cup, and filled the cup with hot coffee.

"Now," she said. "Scrambled eggs. Canadian bacon. Croissants. All right?"

"That sounds wonderful," he said. "I didn't know I was coming for breakfast, but I can't turn it down. Do you mind if I ask some questions while it's on the way?"

"Go ahead, Mr. Shayne." She began breaking eggs into a mixing bowl. "But tell me one thing first. Were those detectives trying to—I don't know quite how to put it—well, intimidate you?"

Shayne grinned again. "They started off with that idea."

"That settles it," she said briskly. "After I told Mr. Painter what I planned to do, he stalked out with a look of black determination on his face. He told me to listen to the twelve o'clock news. I thought that meant he was planning to do something about the Harris case, finally, but apparently he was planning to do something about Michael Shayne!" She glanced at him. "Though I can't imagine how he thought he could get any place with you."

"The only thing he wanted you to do was not to see me till afternoon?"

"He didn't really want me to see you at all. He went off like a Roman candle when I mentioned your name. I probably shouldn't be telling you this." She gave a low laugh. "He was so excited he spilled his drink in his lap."

"I seem to have that effect on Petey," Shayne said.

"He probably doesn't like you to call him Petey either, does he?" When Shayne laughed she went on, "The whole thing was over my head. He said you'd crucify him. That was actually the word he used. But I couldn't change my plans unless he gave me a reason, and that he positively refused to do. He tried to talk me into hiring somebody else, if I insisted on hiring a private detective. The idea being, I suppose, that he wasn't in danger of being crucified by this other man. Well." She poured the beaten eggs into a frying pan. "I'll have to begin by telling you some ancient history."

"I saw the newspaper clips on it yesterday," Shayne said, "but I'd better hear it from you."

She began stirring the eggs with a wooden spoon. "You wouldn't think I'd still have so much trouble talking about it, after three years. But here goes. My husband George worked in the estates department at the Beach Trust. He worked hard, but except during the tax rush every spring he kept regular hours. And it just so happened that one night he had to meet some kind of filing deadline and he worked late. A day earlier or a day later, and he'd still be alive. For some reason that's the thing I can't get out of my mind."

Shayne sipped his hot, aromatic coffee. "Accidents are like that, Mrs. Heminway. He could have been hit by a taxi on the way home."

"I know, I know. And I've got to stop thinking about it. He heard a noise in another part of the building and went to see what it was. It couldn't have been much of a noise, because everything else about the robbery was highly professional. All the alarms were blown out. The watchman had been chloroformed. The vault was cut open neatly and efficiently, and when George, who shouldn't have been in the building at all, suddenly got in the way, the thief shot him, neatly and efficiently.

"I came down to drive George home, and I got there just in time to see somebody walking out of a side entrance with a suitcase. Sam Harris was arrested a few weeks later. He looked like the man I saw. Somebody else saw him as he got into a car, and her identification was more positive than mine. He was convicted. I wanted him to be convicted. It was terrible, how much I wanted it. And when he was found guilty, I wanted him to be sentenced to death."

"That's probably natural," Shayne said.

"Is it?" she said bitterly. "I'm not sure that it is. I'm only sure of one thing—for a long time, too long, I let it poison my life. It changed everything about me. All I could think of was how much I wanted this man to die for leaving me without a husband. Me. To think that some unfeeling murderer could do such a thing to *me!* All I knew about this man Harris was what the newspapers printed about him, and I actually wished I could attend his electrocution and watch them clamp the electrodes on his ankles and behind his ear . . . This is quite a subject for before breakfast."

She gave a sudden cry and snatched the frying pan off the burner. She said ruefully, "I overdid my reaction then, and I've overdone the eggs now. I'll have to start over."

"They look fine to me," Shayne said.

She stirred them doubtfully. "If you're willing to think of it as an omelet—"

She served the eggs and brought a platter of Canadian bacon and a basket of crescent rolls from the warming oven.

"But I got over it," she said. "I won't go into all the stages. I started going to church again, for one thing, and after about a year or so I was able to get to sleep without wishing that some kindly prison official would invite me to throw the switch at Sam Harris's execution. My father moved in with me, and he helped a lot. I started going out with men, and that helped. I even had one or two mild flirtations. I think I'm more or less normal now. But those execution dates—they keep postponing them and postponing them, and it's beginning to seem less and less like Sam Harris's execution and more and more like mine. I don't suppose that will convince you I'm normal. I can't sleep without drugs, or did I say that?"

"Eat," Shayne said gently.

She stared down at her scrambled eggs and picked up her fork. "I think the one thing that kept me sane was that there didn't seem to be any doubt that Harris was guilty. He was caught with a powerful cutting torch and some of the money. He'd already served a long term in prison for bank robbery, and he was known to carry a gun. He claimed that he hadn't done it, but he didn't convince anybody—certainly not me. At the same time, I kept running across stories about cases where eye-witnesses had been positive about an identification, and it turned out later that they had identified the wrong man. And I began to wonder. Could I really be *sure* I had seen Sam Harris, or did I just want to make certain that somebody was punished? Then Norma Harris came to see me."

"That's the wife?"

"Yes. She found a letter that seemed to bear out her husband's story that he was somewhere else that night. The trouble is that it wasn't dated, so by itself it wasn't conclusive. But it was something to start with. Her lawyer's trying to get a stay of execution with it, but it doesn't seem to Norma that he's trying too hard. She took the letter to Painter. He was very hostile and reluctant at first. Then suddenly, for a few days, he seemed to get interested. Then he dropped it again. It seems very strange.

"Norma thinks he's afraid of probing too deeply for fear of finding out that he was responsible for a miscarriage of justice. He's a funny man, and I don't know. Norma asked me to help, and I said I would. And when I went to Painter he acted just as coy with me. Coy's the wrong word. Strange, certainly. He keeps telling us to leave it to him. And day after day goes by, and we still haven't the faintest idea what he's up to, if he's up to anything. Yesterday he wouldn't even let Norma in to see him."

"What's the letter say?"

"Norma has a copy, and you'd better get it from her." She

gave him a direct look. "Does that mean you're taking the case?"

"Hell, yes. I'm just as curious as you are about what Petey's been up to."

She leaned forward impulsively and pressed his hand. "That's wonderful. If you'd turned it down, I'd have to go ahead with an idea Norma has. She wants to call a press conference, where we'd stand up in front of a lot of reporters and cameramen and charge Chief-of-Detectives Peter Painter with deliberate sabotage. I've been dreading it. I'm not the type for that kind of thing. And Norma. We-el, you'll meet her. She gets carried away sometimes, and she might do more harm than good. And my father would really hate it. He practically blew the house down around my ears when I told him I was going to Mr. Painter. You probably don't know—he's Benjamin Chadwick. Does that name—"

Shayne sipped at his coffee, thinking. "President of the Beach Trust."

"He retired last year," she said. "He has a violent aversion to publicity, and it was rather unpleasant in the house for awhile after I put in with Norma Harris. He couldn't understand that it was something I had to do, because of that horrible year when I was eaten up with thoughts of revenge. He couldn't see any point in raking everything up all over again. He was afraid I'd go into another tailspin, as bad as the one I'd finally pulled myself out of. I usually take his advice, but this time I couldn't. Then an awful thing happened. He went to Painter himself, I think to warn him about letting me get too involved. He collapsed on the steps, and he hasn't been able to speak since. He was totally paralyzed for a few days, and he still can't move his left side."

"I'm sorry."

"Well, he's seventy-six. This may sound cruel, but I can't let him put pressure on me. He lies in bed and stares at me, willing me to do what he wants, but I can't."

"Did he tell you he was going to Painter before he went?"

"No, and it was the last thing in the world I expected him

to do. The first thing I knew about it was when they called me. They got his name and address from his driver's license. Mr. Shayne, you know Peter Painter better than I do. What do you think of Norma's theory? That to protect his own reputation, he'd suppress evidence that would cost a man his life?"

Shayne shook his head soberly. "No. Painter wouldn't do that. Is there more coffee?"

"Of course."

She poured more coffee and added cognac. Shayne went on, "But what he's perfectly capable of doing is keeping a piece of evidence in the safe until he can bring it out at the most favorable time, in terms of publicity. He doesn't share your feelings about press conferences. He enjoys them."

"And while he's holding onto this evidence, it wouldn't occur to him that a fellow human being is sitting in a condemned cell, counting the minutes?"

"No, that wouldn't occur to him. He wouldn't class an ex-con as a fellow human being, and that might include the ex-con's wife. On the other hand, maybe the little so-and-so just took it into his head to get stubborn. He doesn't like to be pushed, even by a good-looking widow."

"Thank you, sir," she said.

"You're welcome. But he may have held off too long. It's probably time to tell you that he's missing."

Her hand flew to her throat. "Oh, my God. Missing! You don't mean he's been—that anyone has—"

Shayne shook his head. "Things have to be serious before a cop is deliberately killed, especially when he's a high cop like Painter. It makes for hard feelings. Of course a quarter of a million bucks is a serious sum of money."

"You mean from the robbery?" she said, puzzled. "That's one of Norma's big points. If Sam has it hidden, why doesn't he use some of it to hire a better lawyer? But doesn't this—I know, it's terrible and I certainly hope that nothing has happened to Mr. Painter, but doesn't it show that the truth wasn't brought out at Sam's trial?"

"It probably shows that," Shayne said. "It doesn't mean

that he's innocent. I'll need Norma Harris's address, and the name of that lawyer. And while we're on the subject of money, my secretary keeps telling me to be more businesslike, especially when she's not around to handle it for me. I'll charge you a hundred a day and expenses."

"That's fair enough."

"And I have another incentive besides money. Life wouldn't be the same without Peter Painter."

"I thought you didn't like him."

Shayne's eyebrows went up. "Did I say I *liked* him? I said life wouldn't be the same without him."

She laughed and offered him the coffee pot. When he shook his head she said, "It makes me feel hoggish, leaving your friends outside. If you still have a minute, why don't I see if they'd like a cup of coffee and a roll?"

Shayne stopped with his hands on the edge of the table. "What friends?"

"Didn't you bring two detectives with you?"

"Not that I know of. Don't look out the window. Look at me. I didn't spot them coming out, but they knew where they could find me. I can't operate with cops on my tail, and they ought to know that by now. Can you get me a pocket mirror?"

"I think so." She reached across to a sideboard and rummaged in a purse. "One of them walked past on the other side of the street a few minutes ago. Nobody out here gets up this early, as a rule, and if they do they don't go out for an early morning walk. He got into a parked car down the street, and there's another man in it."

She found a mirror and passed it to him. He was looking out across the bay, his back to the street. He set the mirror on the table, careful to keep the sun from hitting it, and adjusted its angle so he could see the parked cars outside.

"Behind the yellow convertible," she said. "Do you see it?"

"Don't look at the street."

He tilted the mirror and saw a black four-door sedan, probably a Ford. He smiled grimly. "If they want to find out where I'm going from here, I'm going to Beach headquarters. We'll see what their boss has to say. Can you write down those addresses for me? And where will you be if I want to reach you later?"

"I'll be here till the middle of the afternoon, when I go to the nursing home to see Father. I'll put that phone number down, too."

"Fine," Shayne said. "Stay here at the table where they can see you. I'm going to give these boys a fast ride."

She slid him a piece of paper, which he folded and put in his pocket. "I feel better about things, Mr. Shayne. Thanks."

"Mike," he said.

She smiled. "Mike."

He pushed back his chair, moving slowly until he could no longer be seen from the street. An instant later he was out the front door. Cutting across the grass toward his Buick, he leaped in, hit the starter and went back fast. The crushed shells of the driveway spurted from beneath his rear wheels. He cramped the steering wheel sharply as he felt the pavement, reversed and shot forward. He watched the rear-view mirror. He had caught his two friends flat-footed. He went into the climbing turn to the causeway and the black sedan still hadn't moved.

On the causeway he built his speed up rapidly. He slowed at the approaches to the toll station; he still hadn't picked up the sedan in the mirror, and his smile was beginning to fade. He tossed a quarter into the basket, pulled past and stopped in the plaza beyond. When even now the sedan didn't appear, he got out of the Buick and brushed past the toll-collector.

"Can I use your phone?" he said. "Emergency."

"This is no phone booth, Jack," the attendant said.

"It's a local call. Will that cover it?"

He threw the attendant a dollar, which was promptly whisked out of sight. Shayne dialed a number and asked for Lieutenant Wing.

"Wing speaking," a voice said a moment later.

"Shayne," the redhead said abruptly. "You're doing what I asked you not to, Joe. You're crowding me."

"What are you talking about, Mike?"

"Your two boys in the black Ford. I thought at first they were tailing me, but it seems you want somebody to ask Mrs. Heminway the same questions I asked her, to see if you get the same answers. I don't like to be checked up on."

"I still don't know what you're talking about. What two boys in what black Ford? I didn't put anybody on you, Mike, and I didn't send anybody to talk to Mrs. Heminway."

6

THERE WAS A second's pause. Wing said alertly, "Are you still on, Mike? Need some help?"

"I think so," Shayne said slowly, pinching the lobe of his ear. "If we do this right, maybe we can find out something. Get a radio car up to 96th. They'd better hold up at the toll booths. If this black sedan comes through before I'm in position, tell them to grab it. It's a four-door, I'd say two years old, and the first two numbers of the license are seven-three. A Florida tag. Keep the circuit open so they can shoot down to the Heminway house if I need them. Have you got that?"

"Got it, Mike."

Shayne broke the connection, flipped through the book until he found Rose Heminway's number, and dialed it.

"Mrs. Heminway," he said when she answered. "Lock up all around and don't let anybody in, no matter who it is. Do you understand that?"

"But what on earth—"

"Just do it. I'll explain later. Lock up and don't let anybody in."

He hung up. The attendant said, "Shayne, eh?"

"I'll give you my autograph some other time," Shayne said, and ran back to his Buick. He waited approximately fifteen seconds, thinking hard. He could park on the shoulder of the causeway and get back to the island on foot, but that wouldn't accomplish what he had in mind.

He turned left on Collins and took another left to the Haulover Beach charter docks. In a moment he saw a captain he recognized—Jean Prideaux, a Frenchman from Martinique. He left the Buick double-parked with the motor running, and slid a Miami Beach police department courtesy card under the windshield wiper.

Prideau hailed him. "Mike! Not see for months. Come out with me today and kill a sailfish?"

"Not today, Jean. I want some taxi service—ten bucks down to the Bay Harbor islands and back."

The fishing captain looked at him in amazement. "You charter a deep-sea boat to go to *Bay Harbor?*"

"This is business," Shayne said briefly. "I want to sneak up on some people, and they know my car. Fifteen bucks."

"Sure, Mike, sure," Prideaux cried. "Make it quick because I got a party coming."

Shayne jumped in and Prideaux called to a boy at the gas pump, "Tell them I back quick, o.k.?"

"And keep an eye on my car!" Shayne shouted.

Prideaux cast off and gunned the motor. They rocketed away from the dock. Prideaux grinned back at Shayne.

"Noisy, to sneak up on people."

"Take her out past the Haulover and back in," Shayne shouted.

Other fishing boats were heading out toward the Stream with charter parties, and the upper bay was dotted with sails. Prideaux veered to the left, and at a signal from Shayne cut sharply toward the causeway and then swung back toward the islands. The private docks along the water were screened from the single street by palms and hedges. Shayne saw the long, low modern house where he had had breakfast. He let Prideaux pass the dock that went with the house, then signed to him to cut his motor and coast in.

Shayne grabbed at the dock belonging to Rose's next-door neighbor. "Don't tie up," he said in a low voice. "I could be leaving fast."

Prideaux tapped his wrist watch, reminding Shayne that he had paying customers waiting. Shayne stepped onto the dock.

He skirted the boathouse and went across the lawn, parallel to the water's edge. An elderly woman having breakfast alone on the back terrace of the next house looked at him in surprise. He waved cheerfully and went on. As soon as he was hidden behind a flowering hedge, he ran, bent over, to the Heminway house.

He tried the back door. She had done as he had told her; it was locked. He tapped lightly. There was no response from within. As he moved off the small porch and started along the back of the house he could hear the electric pump hammering in the basement. All the windows on that side of the house were shut and locked, and an air-conditioning unit was sealed into a bedroom window. He reached the single frosted glass window of the bathroom. The shower was running. He tapped sharply on the glass with his fingernail, but the noise of the shower drowned it out. He went to the corner of the house and looked around carefully.

The black sedan had moved up in front of the house. The front door was open. Shayne could see only one of the two men. He was sitting sideways in the front seat, his feet on the curb. Shayne's eyes closed down to slits. He didn't like this man's looks. He was overweight for his height, with heavy jowls and a thick neck. He hadn't shaved yet this morning, and he needed it badly. The stubble was grayish and dirty-looking. His hat was pushed back on his head. He had a loose, careless look, as though nothing mattered to him.

Shayne pulled back, moving slowly so he wouldn't attract the man's eye. He thought for a moment and went back to the bathroom window. Taking a half dollar from his pocket, he clinked it against the glass. It sounded very loud to Shayne's ears, but it didn't seem to penetrate the noise of the shower. He flicked open a pen-knife. Reaching up to his full height, he slipped the blade through the crack between the upper and lower sash and forced the catch. Then he raised the lower sash just enough so he could work his fingers beneath the bottom. He raised it without difficulty.

"Mrs. Heminway," he whispered. "Rose."

He heard a noise from the front of the house and sprang up, getting the upper half of his rangy body in across the sill. He wriggled headfirst into the bathroom and came down on his hands. He had just turned to close the window when the shower went off and Rose Heminway opened the door of the shower stall.

She gasped and raised one hand, as though to hold him off. "*Michael Shayne!*"

He was still in a slight crouch, breathing hard from the exertion. Her hair was pinned up on the top of her head, to get it out of the water's way. The first thing Shayne noticed was that she was very clean, but that wasn't all he noticed. He would have to report to Lucy Hamilton what had happened in Miami while she was in New Orleans, but on the whole, he thought, he had better not tell her he had climbed in through a bathroom window.

"It's all right," he said reassuringly. "It's the only way I could get in. Those guys in front aren't cops."

One hand fluttered to her forehead and she reached out with the other for something solid to hold onto. "Mike, I feel so—"

"Don't faint!" Shayne said sharply. "There's no time for that. Here."

He grabbed a large towel from the nearest rack and held it out. Her eyelids trembled. She tried to say something, but her breath came out in a sigh and she fell forward. He caught her under the arms, suppressing the profanity that sprang to his lips, and dragged her to the bedroom. He laid her on the bed, wet as she was, and towelled her roughly. She was only unconscious a moment. The cool air of the bedroom brought her back. She sat up and seized the towel.

"Just what do you think you're trying to—" she began indignantly, but he cut her off with a peremptory gesture.

"No, Rose. That's another thing there's no time for."

He saw her red robe thrown over the back of a chair. He got it for her. "Put this on. Never mind about getting dry first. Put it on. Right away, please."

She put an arm into one sleeve, still trying to hold the towel

"*Come in*," Rose called more loudly. "It's not locked."

The man pushed the door open and looked in. "Mrs. Heminway?"

"Put it down anywhere," Rose called. "How much do I owe you?"

He came a step into the room, holding the doorknob. Rose swung around on the low bench, and her breath caught. The quick movement pulled the robe further off her shoulder. Shayne, watching the man's face, saw it change.

"I thought you were the cleaners," she said. "Come in and shut the door. I've got the air-conditioning on, and you're warming up the house.

She gave him a slow, provocative look, accompanied by a slight smile. Her breast had almost escaped entirely from the robe. "I don't think I know you, do I? But do come in. I hate to shout."

The man touched his bottom lip with his tongue and swallowed. He held up one finger, signing to his friend that he would only be a minute. He took off his hat and let the door swing shut.

"Are you selling something?" Rose said gayly, and went on without waiting for a reply, "I know this is unconventional, but I want to finish brushing my hair. Come in and give me your sales talk."

The man approached the door, holding his hat in front of him. "My name's Cole. I wanted to find out if your father's name was Chadwick? If you used to be married to George Heminway?"

"Why, yes! Did you know George? I don't think I ever heard him mention anybody named Cole."

"We were old friends."

Now the open door concealed him from Shayne, but the redhead knew from his tone that he was watching the reflection in the mirror. Shayne was watching it himself. She leaned forward as though to adjust a slipper. The voice on the other side of the door sounded strained.

"Jesus, I'd like nothing better than to kill a little time here, but I'd be taking a hell of a chance, no matter how you look at it."

"What are you babbling about, Mr. Cole?"

Cole took another step forward. "I hate like hell to do this to a dish like you, baby, but that's how it is."

He moved his hat, and Shayne saw a pistol, a long-snouted Lüger, equipped with a silencer. His shoulder lifted slightly, and his jaw muscles tightened.

Without conscious thought, Shayne chopped at his arm and spun him around. Cole must have caught the movement in the mirror, for he was already turning, trying to bring the gun between them. Shayne stepped in fast, hitting him with a hard low left to the body. He started to crumble, and as his head sagged forward the redhead clubbed him with a right behind the ear.

The gun thudded to the floor. Cole went down to both knees. His head rocked backward, his eyes showing only the whites. Shayne caught himself before his follow-through could take him off-balance, and came back with a slashing downward left that met Cole's jaw forward of the hinge. There was a crisp little click of contact. They wouldn't be bothered with Cole for some time to come.

Shayne caught him before he was all the way down, turned him and got his wallet. He looked up. Rose was still sitting at the dressing table with a hairbrush in her hand.

"Adhesive tape," he said. "Quick. As much as you've got."

There was over five hundred dollars in the wallet. Shayne left the money alone and shucked the cards and papers on the floor. The man's name, if his driving license could be believed, was actually Cole, Albert Cole. He was a member of the Diner's Club and Carte Blanche, and he had a union card, a credit card entitling him to friendly treatment at a chain of gas stations, and pictures of two young children. The only thing Shayne learned in the quick once-over was that his last address had been Baltimore.

Then Rose was back with two spools of adhesive tape. Shayne taped Cole's wrists, ankles and mouth. He left him on the floor and picked up the gun, a murderous weapon which would have blown a hole through the wall. He snapped on the safety.

"No fooling this time, Rose," he said. "Who is he?"

Except for her lips, her face had lost all its color. She was staring with horror at the gun.

"I don't know! Mike!" she cried as the realization broke through. "He was going to shoot me!"

"That's how it looked," Shayne said grimly, taking off the silencer.

Her knuckles were pressed against her mouth. "*What have I got myself into, Mike?*"

"That's what we'd all like to know. I think it's going to turn out that killing people is this guy's business. Why would anybody want to kill you?"

She made a helpless gesture. "I can't even begin to guess. I'm the original innocent bystander, Mike. All I did was go to the police to find out why they weren't taking any action on Norma's letter."

Shayne looked at her for a moment, then went to the phone and dialed the number of Beach headquarters. "Joe Wing," he snapped, and to Rose: "Have you ever fired a gun?"

Her eyes widened. "No. You don't mean you want me to shoot—"

"No, no," Shayne said, and spoke into the phone. "Joe. I'm in a hurry, and this has to be done right. I need five minutes. Is your squad car in position?"

"Yeah, do you want it?"

"Not yet. Five minutes from now I want them to turn on their siren, good and loud. Keep that up another minute, and then come down to the island. Mrs. Heminway has somebody we want you to look at."

"How about the Ford?"

"Let it go by. I want to see where it goes."

He slammed down the phone. He held out the Lüger, and Rose took it gingerly in both hands. The long barrel was trembling.

"Point it the other way!" Shayne said. "This guy outside is just the wheel-man, and I think he'll stay in the car and try to be patient. If he tries to get in, shoot him."

"I couldn't any more shoot anybody, Mike—"

"There's nothing to it. The safety's off. Just point it and pull the trigger. When you hear the siren, fire twice out the bathroom window. This is a bottleneck here, and he'll want to get out of it in a hurry."

"But Mike—"

He gave her a reassuring wink and let himself out the back door.

7

CAPTAIN PRIDEAUX saw him coming at a run, and had the motor turning over when he reached the boat. They left the dock in a long easy curve, the engine throttled down all the way. Other boats were passing, one with a noisy outboard, and in another moment Shayne thought it was safe to open up.

He nodded to Prideaux, and the powerful boat shot toward its home pier. The redhead checked the time as they went, wondering if five minutes was cutting it too close. Prideaux cut the power and brought the boat in along the charter docks, and at that moment Shayne heard the siren from the causeway. He leaped onto the dock and sprinted for his Buick.

A minute or so later he was pulling into the plaza at the end of the causeway. He made a full U-turn, ending up pointing away from the bay. He could follow the wail of the siren as the police car raced along the causeway and down onto the Bay Harbor islands. When the black Ford showed up in the line of traffic, coming fast, Shayne eased forward and parked.

He unfolded a road map. He had his face behind it when the Ford pulled past him. Shayne threw the map aside and followed. A Pontiac, leaving the toll station, crowded in ahead of him, but it didn't matter. Scared by the shots and the siren, the Cuban in the Ford was taking his time, keeping within the speed limit.

He made the turn onto Collins. Shayne kept him in view, without doing anything to attract attention himself. On Dade Boulevard, the Ford dropped out of the traffic and parked near a large drugstore. The Cuban was careful to feed the parking meter after leaving the car. Shayne pulled up in an open space by a fire hydrant, and when the Cuban went into the drugstore, Shayne got out, unlocked his trunk and opened a suitcase he kept there for occasions like this one.

He took off his checked jacket and replaced it with an inconspicuous gray tweed. He had a light straw hat in the back seat, and he put this on. As soon as a legal parking slot opened up ahead of him, he moved into it, after which he strolled past the drugstore, spotted the Cuban leaving a phone booth inside, and went back to the Buick.

Then he waited.

A few minutes passed. The Cuban emerged and went to the corner of Alton Road, where he stepped off the curb and began waving at taxis. An empty cab slowed for him. Timing his moves, Shayne was the second car behind the taxi as it went along Collins and some minutes later turned in at the St. Albans, one of the big new hotels. The Cuban thrust a bill at his driver and walked briskly through the revolving door. Shayne knew the doorman here. He jammed on the emergency brake.

"Take care of it, will you, Frank?" he said, giving the man a dollar. "And I may want to put my hands on it in a hurry."

"Sure, Mr. Shayne."

Shayne went into the vast modernistic lobby, under the golden dome. This was the tail-end of the tourist season and the big conventions were underway; the St. Albans was usually rented to capacity at this time of year. Shayne began to circle, looking for the Cuban.

"Mike!" somebody called.

Shayne waved amiably and pushed through the crowd. He spotted the Cuban waiting for an elevator with several short, fleshy men, each of them wearing a large lapel badge shaped like a truck-tire. The Cuban had seen Shayne run out of Mrs. Heminway's house, and though he had had only that one rapid glimpse, the detective didn't want to use the same elevator. There was no way it could be avoided, however, and he crowded in with the rest, letting his shoulders slump and keeping his chin in against his chest. There were no women in the car, and he kept his hat on. This elevator served the floors from ten to fifteen, and the Cuban got off at twelve. Three others got off with him, one of them Michael Shayne.

There were more of the big lapel badges in the corridor, and Shayne had had a chance to study one in the elevator. These were delegates to the convention of the I.U.D.T.H., initials which stood for International Union of Draymen, Truckers and Handlers. As Shayne followed the Cuban, his thoughts were busy. Albert Cole, who had been pointing a gun at Rose Heminway just before the ceiling fell in on him, had carried a membership card in this same union, which was noted, among other things, for the ex-convicts among its organizers and officials. Apparently the entire 12th floor had been taken over by the delegates, and not many had brought their wives. From the looks of things, Shayne wasn't the only one here who had been up all night.

Three delegates came out of a room with drinks in their hands. They were friendly, in fact over-friendly, and they wanted the redhead to join a quartette to sing the old favorites. By the time Shayne untangled himself the Cuban was gone.

There were three doors he might have used. The first was locked. Shayne tried the next. A man wearing pajama bottoms sat up in bed and roared, "Get out of here! I want a little privacy!" The woman in bed with him giggled. Shayne retreated and tried the next room.

This was the sitting room of a one-bedroom suite. There were four men in shirt sleeves sitting around a low coffee table. They all had drinks. One was thumbing through a card-index. Another, with a sheaf of papers attached to a clip-board, seemed to be checking names.

They all looked at Shayne.

"They don't knock around here?" one of them said.

"Looking for a friend of mine," Shayne said, and started for the bedroom.

One of the men got up so fast his chair went over. He had a large bald head, but his features were crowded together near the middle of his face, with not enough space between them. His shoulders and chest bulked very large.

"Uh-uh," he said.

Shayne smiled agreeably and kept going.

"Who is this mouser?" the man with the clipboard said.

"Hell, it's Mike Shayne!"

The fourth man hooted. Getting up off the sofa, he gave the redhead a friendly blow on the muscle of his nearest arm. He was built close to the ground, broad, compact, and as solid as a truck, and until Shayne caught the blow on his muscle he hadn't recognized him. This had been an old habit of Harry Plato, who had just put in a turbulent two-year term as president of the international. He had changed since Shayne saw him last. His hair was snow-white and his face had been deeply seared by time and trouble.

"I forgot you operated in this town, Mike," he said. "Long time no see, huh? This is Shayne, the private badge," he explained. "A good guy. Maybe he don't look it, but plenty of stuff up there under that red fuzz. He handled a case for me once when I had the New Orleans district. Earned a nice piece of scratch for himself, as I recall. What brings you, Mike? You wouldn't be looking for business, by any chance?"

"Have you got some for me?" Shayne said, looking past him into the bedroom.

"I'll always find a spot for a good man. Who's this friend you're looking for?"

"Al Cole," Shayne said.

There was no visible reaction among the four men, but Shayne thought they were being too careful not to look at him. He went on, "But I shouldn't have said he was a friend. The last I heard, he was lugging a gun around Baltimore. I can see I've got the wrong room. See you around, Harry."

"I'll be here all week," Plato said heartily. "Drop in and I'll buy you a drink. And if I can assist you with anything, anything at all, just say the word, Mike."

"I'll do that, Harry," Shayne said, stepping back. "While I'm here, mind if I use your bathroom?"

Plato moved to intercept him, and his hand closed on Shayne's arm. "Be my guest. But now I remember something else about you, Mike. You never refused a drink, no matter if it was before breakfast or what. Whizzer," he said to the bald man who had blocked Shayne when he came into the room. "Get my pal here a little of that hundred-proof medicine in a tall glass without much water."

"Some other time, Harry," Shayne said, looking down at the fingers wrapped around his arm. "And if you're remembering things about me, maybe you remember I don't like to be handled."

"Now," Plato said. "Don't get offended so easy, Mike. This is one of those habits with me. I see somebody I like, I just sort of naturally grab hold."

He let go. Shayne went into the empty bedroom. The bathroom was also empty, but there was a door from the bedroom to the corridor, and by now the Cuban had had plenty of time to use it. The redhead returned to the sitting room. Plato came to the door with him.

"Sure you won't change your mind and have that drink?"

"Yeah," Shayne growled. "How long have you been down in Miami?"

"Couple of days." He groaned and clasped his head. "It's a rat race, Mike, and I'm getting out of it. Did you hear that yet?"

"Out of the union?"

Plato laughed, and barely kept himself from slapping Shayne's shoulder. "I'm not a rich man, for God's sake. Can I retire at my age? I'm running for top dog in the Welfare Fund, and I can't see any reason why I shouldn't get it. I've had enough of this president merry-go-round. The headaches! You wouldn't believe it if I told you. This is one tough outfit, Mike, and I want to tell you it's like trying to stay on a pair of waterskis when you're tied to three different boats. I've aged in this office. I don't know if you noticed?"

He looked at Shayne hopefully, expecting to be told that he looked as young as ever. Shayne said bluntly, "I hardly recognized you, Harry."

"Oh," Plato said, disappointed. "Well, is it so surprising? Those newspaper jerks. You'd think I was Al Capone, Jr., or somebody. And those Senators! Who are they, God Almighty? Two years is about all I can take."

He followed Shayne to the corridor, where he looked around carefully and lowered his voice. "What are you looking for Cole for?" he said in a serious tone, with none of his earlier false joviality. "And how come up here?"

"I thought I saw him," Shayne said. "He was with a dark-haired guy, a little mustache, maybe a Cuban. He went into one of the rooms along here."

"Is this—well, frankly, I'd appreciate it a lot if you'd tell me, because the beanballs they keep throwing at me, I've got to be ready to bail out. Is it union business?"

"Not as far as I know, Harry. But he belongs to one of your Baltimore locals, and it's lousy public relations to have people at your convention carrying Lügers. It gives the public the wrong idea."

"Well, if Cole is carrying a gun," Plato said carefully, "and I don't know why the hell he should be, he probably has a permit."

"Maybe in Baltimore," Shayne said. "Not in Miami. And they don't give out permits for silencers, even in Baltimore. But don't worry about it, Harry. I took it away from him."

The marks on Plato's face deepened. "Don't worry about it! I'm worrying about it, don't worry. This kind of headline is all we need." He lowered his voice still further. "Did anybody get shot with it?"

"Luckily, no," Shayne said. "When you say you've been having trouble, have you had any with Peter Painter?"

"With who?"

"Painter, Chief-of-Detectives here on the Beach."

"Oh, yeah, he's the guy you keep having those run-ins with. I read about it somewhere. No, I haven't been bothered by any of the local cops this trip, knock on wood. Do you want to tell me why you ask that question?"

"I don't think so, Harry. When's the convention start?"

"We come to order at—" He looked at his big watch, from which, if he wished, he could also learn the day and the date. "Jesus, we came to order fifteen minutes ago. I ought to get down there, not that much happens today. Tomorrow's our big day, elections. Now I've got to operate, Mike. I've got a screwy feeling, and I wish I didn't have it, that you and I are going to be in touch."

He was about to open the door when Tim Rourke came charging up the corridor, calling, "Harry! Mr. Plato!"

To his friend Michael Shayne, Rourke looked as though he had just crawled out of a compost heap. He was never exactly dapper, but today his clothes had a slept-in look, which was probably deserved. His eyes were being held open with difficulty. His long bony fingers trembled. His face was the color of ashes, and his voice came out in a hoarse croak.

Harry Plato looked at him in disgust. "What do you want?"

"Give me a minute, give me a minute," Rourke said. "Collect my thoughts. And as for *you*, Mike. That's kind of a high point, giving a guy as a character reference at four in the morning."

"Five," Shayne said, grinning.

Plato looked from the reporter to Shayne. "You know this poison-pen artist, Mike?"

"Don't call me names," Rourke begged. "Usually I just shrug it off, but I'm not up to witty repartee this morning. Harry, what's this about you and Luke Quinn? I hear he's supporting somebody else for the big money job."

"Wait till the votes are counted," Plato said coldly.

"Do you want me to quote you that there's nothing to it?"

"I don't want to say a goddam word to you, jerk," Plato said.

He stalked back into the room and slammed the door. Rourke winced at the sound.

"Why does everybody have to *shout?*" he said.

"I thought you'd report sick this morning," Shayne said. "But here you are, bright and cheerful, hard at work as usual."

"Don't give me that, you bastard. What about this four-in-the-morning jazz? When somebody calls up and says a friend of mine claims he spent the night at my place, naturally I'll back him up. I expect him to do the same for me. But what was so goddam urgent it couldn't wait till a decent hour?"

"Tim," Shayne said patiently, "nobody was asking you to perjure yourself. I did spend the night at your place, or most of it. We played poker, remember?"

"Sure we played poker. But if you think I can tell you who was there most of the time, you've got the wrong idea about the evening, kid. Hold it. Don't disappear. *It's important.*"

He walked away from Shayne, slipping between two knots of Trucker delegates, and cut off a tall, ruddy-faced man of about thirty-five, who was too well dressed to be anything but a union official. He wore dark-rimmed glasses, a preoccupied expression, and a conservative suit with a small stripe, which Shayne guessed had retailed at several hundred dollars. His breast pocket handkerchief was carefully folded.

Shayne heard Rourke call, "Can I have a minute, Mr. Quinn?"

The redhead went down the hall. The next door after Harry Plato's was locked. The door after that was marked with a red light, and led to the concrete fire-stairs. He returned to Rourke.

"Okay, okay," Rourke was saying impatiently. "Play it cagey. I understand things are subject to change and you don't want to commit yourself. But if something breaks, will you call me? You're a local boy, and that ought to mean something. Don't give it to the wire services first, give it to us and *we'll* give it to the wire services. Anything you want in the way of pictures we'll supply, within reason. You'll get better space that way."

"That's good of you, Tim," Quinn said, in a surprisingly gravelly voice. "But it's delicate, you know?"

He glanced at Shayne, nodded and moved on.

Shayne said irritably, "I don't know what I'm doing, and you know better than to push me, Tim. I tailed somebody here and lost him."

"You lost him?" Rourke made a superior sound with his tongue. "I didn't know that happened to Mike Shayne."

"It happens," Shayne said.

"How chintzy are you going to be with me?" Rourke said after a moment, peering at him suspiciously. "I don't print everything I hear, for God's sake. There isn't room in the paper. Are you going to tell me what's going on, or are you going to be a real son of a bitch? In which case, the hell with you, and when Lucy gets back I'll tell her I had to give you an alibi for the hours between midnight and four a.m."

Shayne laughed. "You don't have to go that far. I'm working for a lady named Rose Heminway, and don't ask me what she was doing between midnight and four, because I don't know. Did you read those clips you got out of the morgue for me yesterday?"

"Read them? I wrote them . . . No, I know what you mean, and anything you're interested in, I'm interested in too. So I refreshed my recollection. Rose Heminway would be the dead man's widow, right? What's she want to do, take back the identification?"

"Something like that," Shayne said. "And you can't expect Painter to like it. But talk to Wing. I don't know how much they want to give out right now."

Rourke squinted at Shayne. "And the tie-up with the Truckers?"

"That I really don't know, Tim, and there's a lot more I don't know. I only took the case a couple of hours ago."

Rourke finished his drink in two long swallows. He shuddered. "Well, that's a little better, but I still don't feel human. How do I look?"

"You don't look human, either."

"Compliments. That's what I need in the shape I'm in. I was planning to spend the day with these guys, making contacts and drinking their booze, but now I don't know. I don't like the Painter angle. I hope he keeps the hell away from this convention, because anything he's in on gets bolloxed for fair. And I'd really like to get this story. Plato's running for head of the Welfare Fund. That's not supposed to be public knowledge yet."

"He just broke it to me."

"Do you know how much dough there is in that fund? There's so many goddam zeroes it looks like the Federal budget. When you're playing around with something that size, and when you don't have too many scruples to start with, and when you've got a loyal membership that figures you deserve a little gravy after all your hard work, and they'd take just as much if they happened to be in your thirty-buck shoes —well, that's a job there's some percentage in battling over."

"Plato's got his heart set on it. Not that he didn't do okay as president. Big house, big car, big boat. But big trouble to go with it, especially since these Senators have been nipping at him. Why, the way things are going, Mike, people are getting the idea, God forbid, that he's no better than a crook. He wants a little peace and quiet, and he thinks he'll get it, along with a few extra bucks, in the Welfare Fund. Right now it's touch and go. Maybe he'll make it, maybe not."

"Where's Luke Quinn come in?"

"Plato needs Quinn's backing to put him over. That's the way I hear it, and I've got a couple of pretty good contacts in the so-called rank and file. There's a dozen different districts in the union, all with their own favorite sons. The wheeling and the dealing lately has been fierce. You stick a knife in the man from New England, you buy off the man from the Southwest, you wheedle, you charm, you promise, you use your muscle. Get the general picture?"

Shayne was worrying his earlobe. "And if Quinn backs him, Plato's in?"

"That's about it. There's a rank-and-filer in the argument and they're letting him stay in, so people will know what a democratic union this is. There's one real candidate besides Plato, from the West Coast. Whichever way Quinn leans, that man's got it. So Quinn is being wooed. This is the situation that gets me up here when I would rather be convalescing in a comfortable bed from late hours and too much bourbon. Because how do you woo somebody like Quinn? He's only been in the upper echelons a couple of years, so you can't promise to get him one of the top jobs. He's got to mature first. You can't use muscle on him, because he's got muscle of his own, and plenty of it. What would you suggest, Mr. Shayne?"

"Money," Shayne said.

"Money is the correct answer," Rourke said. "You've been coached. That's what my sources say, anyhow. Mike, if I could get the real lowdown on what's happening here, and prove it, honest to God—it wouldn't just be local news. It'd make page one in every paper in the country. Of course," he added, "I don't want to get the story and end up on the obituary page in the same day's paper. I keep telling myself to be careful. Some of these guys give me goose pimples, or is that melodramatic? . . . I need another drink"

8

THEY WENT BACK to the corridor. Rourke went looking for a friendly delegate who would fill his glass. Shayne took the elevator to the lobby, where he shut himself in a phone booth and dialed Beach headquarters. Joe Wing seemed to be glad to hear from him.

"Have you got him, Mike?"

"No, he slipped me," Shayne said. "His Ford's in front of a drugstore just off the causeway on Collins."

"Not any more. We just towed it in. It was stolen last night at International Airport, and one of the boys spotted the tags. We're trying to raise fingerprints, but everything's pretty smudged."

"He took a cab to the St. Albans from there," Shayne said, "and he got away from me on the twelfth floor. The place is running over with truckers in for the big convention, if that means anything."

"Uh-oh," Wing said, and went on slowly, "Al Cole, the boy you gift-wrapped for us, pays dues in that union. I've been talking to Baltimore. He has a medium-long sheet. Five or six arrests, a couple of small convictions. What did you hit him with, Mike?"

"I didn't like the looks of that silencer," Shayne said. "It surprised the hell out of me, and I nearly lost a client. That's something I hate to do. I was afraid for a minute I'd broken my hand. But it seems to be okay."

"Maybe your hand is okay," Wing said dryly, "but he's going to be eating through a straw for the next few weeks. He also won't be doing much talking. Did you get anything more on Painter? You may not believe this, but I'm beginning to worry about the twerp."

"I get an impression, for what it's worth, that he was onto something and he tried to squeeze it too hard. I want to see Norma Harris. She's probably not talking to the Beach police these days, but there's no reason she wouldn't talk to me. Outside of that, I can't see anything to do but try to retrace Petey's footsteps the last couple of weeks."

Wing sighed. "I was hoping this would turn out to be something simple. How are you going to trace his footsteps if he didn't leave any? He must have been afraid of a leak in the department. That's the only way I can explain it. I've been checking his schedule, starting with the day Norma Harris came to see him. It's full of gaps. He was out of the office a lot, but he didn't tell anybody where he was going or why. He did his phoning from a booth, and that's not like Painter—he's a man who liked to hang onto his dimes."

"How about after what's-his-name started driving him? Heinemann?"

"Well, he's a little dim, Mike, if you didn't notice. A perfectly good cop, but he doesn't do any more thinking than he has to. We've been talking about it. I was tired to begin with, and a lot tireder when I finished. I'll go through my notes on what he told me and see if anything points to the Truckers. Do you want to call me back?"

"No, I'll hold on."

Shayne waited, drumming impatiently on the wall of the booth.

Wing exclaimed, "Here's something. I knew the St. Albans rang a bell. Painter went there the day before yesterday. He talked to somebody on the house phone and went up in the elevator. He was gone a half hour."

"Did Heinemann notice what floor?"

"That's just the sort of thing he doesn't think he's being paid to notice. I know there's something else here, if I can find it."

Again Shayne waited. He put down the phone and started a cigarette.

"Yeah," Wing said finally. "Not that it's much. Heinemann's not sure when this was, sometime last week. He drove Painter to a very crummy bowling alley, somewhere in the neighborhood of Eighth, called the Three Hundred Club. Painter checked his .38 before they went in. It's that kind of joint. Heinemann stuck with him to the manager's office, and then he stayed outside and watched the door. The name is Horvath, Sticky Horvath. I looked up his record, and it's not good. He served two jolts for receiving stolen goods, and he was mentioned in that loan shark investigation a few years back. Remember, Mike? Nothing came of it in the way of prosecution, but Horvath was supposed to have a corner on the loan-sharking in the Truckers local."

"Painter didn't tell anybody why he wanted to talk to him?"

"Not a word. That might be something for you, Mike. A guy like Horvath doesn't talk to us unless we have something to hit him with. But you better let us backstop you."

"No, that might queer it," Shayne said. "I'll see what happens. How's Mrs. Heminway?"

"Pretty shaky. She thinks you're hot stuff, incidentally. Everything's quiet over there, and I left a man with her to be sure it stays quiet."

"One other thing," Shayne said. "Tim Rourke's going to be calling you. His paper knows that something's up, and you can't sit on the story much longer. He might be willing to hold off if you give him an exclusive deal, but not for long."

"Thanks, Mike. I'll see if I can stall him. Keep moving in. I've got a hunch we might be on the edge of something."

Shayne hung up. He had a surprising feeling of let-down, of incompleteness, as though something important was missing. It took him a moment to put his finger on what it was. It was Painter. Given a choice between a hard-working, hard-driving, intelligent cop like Joe Wing, and an irrational, infuriating bundle of contradictions like Peter Painter, only a total fool would choose Painter. But without Painter to rail at and out-maneuver, there was no doubt that some of the keen enjoyment Shayne usually got from an intricate case like this was simply not there. He smiled ruefully, but the smile left his deeply lined face as he threated his way through the crowded lobby. What had *happened* to the little son of a bitch?

The doorman whistled up Shayne's car. The redhead threw away his cigarette and stuck another in his mouth. He left it unlighted. It was still there some ten minutes later when he cruised slowly up and down the streets in the honkeytonk section at the southern end of the Beach, until he found the Three Hundred Club, an establishment which compared unfavorably with the luxury hotel he had just left.

Cars left unattended in this part of town had a way of losing hubcaps, radio aerials and sometimes wheels. Shayne continued till he found a garage and walked back. At this hour the neighborhood had a dejected air, with the strip-joints and bars still padlocked and most of the neon lights turned off. The front door of the Three Hundred Club was open, but there didn't seem to be much activity inside.

The unwashed windows didn't allow much sunlight to enter, and the lights were on. Five or six loungers were reading the morning paper, studying scratch sheets, and waiting for the morning to pass. They were all male, all under twenty. They were wearing the uniform of their age-group, T-shirts and blue jeans, and one had a leather cap with union dues-buttons on its broken peak.

Shayne paused inside the door to light his cigarette and give everyone a chance to get adjusted to a new arrival.

"No school today, boys?" he said.

One of the youths sneered. That was the only response. They went on with what they were doing, but Shayne knew that he had their attention. He addressed the one in the leather cap.

"Sticky in yet?"

"What do you want to see him for?"

"Guess," Shayne said, and walked into the alleys, none of

which were being used. The youth in the leather cap came along with him, walking fast.

"He's busy. Who do I say wants to see him?"

Looking around, Shayne saw a door marked PRIVATE, *No Admittance*. He sauntered toward it. The youth scrambled around in front of him.

"Cool it," he said warningly. "He always wants to know who somebody is. That's the way we do it around here."

Shayne grinned and kept coming. The boy held his ground until Shayne was only a stride away, but he didn't seem to care for what he saw in the redhead's face. He began to fall back. "Listen—"

Shayne grazed him as he went by. He tapped on the door with the private label.

"You see?" he said. "Nothing to get excited about. I'm being polite."

"Come in," a voice called.

Shayne opened the door. The man behind the cluttered desk was nearly as grubby as his place of business, and that was very grubby. He was wearing a full beard, and he had a real loan shark's eyes. He was sipping coffee from a thick crockery cup without a handle. He looked at the youth in the leather cap.

"Who do we have here, lame-brain, and why?"

Shayne came on into the room. There was a small battered safe on the floor, its door ajar.

"I want to go on being polite," he said, "but I don't like to be the only one. This is no way to do business. Maybe I want to borrow some money."

"This ain't a bank," Horvath said.

"That's not what I heard."

Shayne reached toward his hip for his wallet. Horvath froze, his hands below the level of the desk. The redhead laughed.

"If you're that nervous about your assets, close your goddam safe."

He held out his open wallet and let Horvath see his private investigator's license. Horvath lifted his hands into sight again.

"This is an honor," he said sarcastically. "If you want to bowl, you can have the first game on the house."

"That's not the side of your business I'm interested in," Shayne said. "Let's have the kid wait outside."

After a moment Horvath moved his head, and the boy faded back out of the doorway and closed the door.

"Now what?" Horvath said.

Shayne cleared off a corner of the desk and sat down. "I'm trying to get a line on a cop here in town. His name's Peter Painter, one of our leading citizens. I've had him on my back for years. I made him look bad on a case once, and he's been trying to ruin me ever since. He's come close a few times, and I've been looking for a way to put him out of circulation."

"I'm supposed to get worked up about this?"

"A scandal would do it," Shayne went on calmly. "I got a tip from a friend in the neighborhood that he came to see you last week. I hope none of your boys tried to steal the hubcaps off his Caddy, because that kind of thing makes Painter sore. Now let's take a hypothetical case. Say he's in a jam and he has to raise money in a hurry. He doesn't want to bother his friends, such as they are. It's not the kind of jam he can explain to a bank. What would be more natural than to visit his friendly neighborhood loan shark?"

"And how awful for him if anybody found out," Horvath said with mock sympathy.

"Exactly," Shayne said. "If I knew how much he had to raise, maybe I could find out why he had to raise it. I'm still trying to be polite, but he wouldn't come here unless it was something he wouldn't want to get out."

"What was that name, Painter?" Horvath said, pretending to consider.

"I don't expect you to recognize it for nothing. I'll go as high as a hundred."

Horvath caressed his beard. "A hundred wouldn't even begin to—"

Shayne interrupted. "A hundred's the price for this information. That's high, as you know as well as I do. Come on, Sticky. I've got other calls."

"Let's see the hundred."

Shayne took two fifties out of that compartment of his wallet and showed them to him. It was clear that Horvath wished they were his.

"He didn't want a loan," he said reluctantly. "The subject didn't come up."

"What did he want?"

Horvath forced his eyes away from the bills, giving them up with a sigh. "If he came here at all, and remember I'm not admitting a damn thing, he probably wanted to sell me a ticket to a cop's benefit or something. I gave him a quick brush."

Shayne returned the bills to his wallet. "You don't want to think twice about that answer?"

"I already thought three times. I'm in business. I want to go on being in business at this location. Hell, I told you he didn't try to borrow any dough, didn't I? That ought to be worth fifty."

Shayne put out his cigarette on the surface on the desk. It wasn't the first cigarette that had been put out there.

"It's not even worth a beer," he said. "Let's back away and try something else. I hear you've been slammed a few times for receiving. Do you ever take a chance on big denomination bills or negotiable securities?"

"Be serious, Shayne," he said uneasily. "Do I look it?"

"I guess not. How about your exclusive with the Truckers? Did Petey go into that?"

His eyes jumped. The corner of his mouth may have twitched, but it was hidden by the big beard. "That's all, Shayne. Out."

"Did you ever loan Sam Harris any money?"

Immediately the loan-shark eyes were alert and watchful. "The guy who gets the charge this week? Is that why you want to know about hot bills?" He touched his beard thoughtfully. "They never found all that loot, did they?"

Shayne grinned down at him wolfishly. "Only about twenty grand. Does that give you any ideas?"

Horvath waited for another instant, then made up his mind. "Out. I happen to have work to do."

"I'll say it once more," Shayne said easily. "I'm not asking you to blow the whistle on anybody. I just want to know what questions Painter asked you. You don't have to tell me the answers, just the questions, for an easy hundred bucks."

"*O-u-t*," Horvath said, his voice climbing.

Reaching out, he stabbed a button on his desk. A bell clanged outside in the bowling alleys. The door opened but Shayne didn't look around.

"Throw him out," Horvath said curtly.

The redhead went on looking down at him, then stooped, took hold of the legs of the heavy desk and heaved it up and over. It landed in Horvath's lap.

"Grab the son of a bitch!" Horvath yelled hysterically. "Grab him."

The boy in the leather cap had been joined by two others. Shayne went toward them at a leisurely walk. A path opened for him. Horvath screamed, "Crack his skull! Knock the goddam teeth out of his head!" Then more frantically: "Get this goddam thing off me!"

Shayne went through the door and closed it behind him. The three boys kept a pace away, shuffling uneasily.

The youth in the leather cap said, "Hurry it up, will you?"

"Aren't you going to throw me out?" Shayne said.

"Well, you're going anyway, why make a production out of it? When you first came in, I didn't know you were Mike Shayne."

Shayne went through the waiting room. Behind him, one of the boys took a bowling ball out of the rack and began slamming it against the cinderblock wall. Another boy groaned.

Shayne returned to the garage and paid for his car.

9

NORMA HARRIS HAD A walk-up apartment on the Miami side of the bay. A moment or two after Shayne rang her doorbell, the lobby door opened and a dark-haired woman came out. She glanced at Shayne as she passed, turning back as she reached the outer door.

"You didn't just ring Harris?"

"Yeah. Are you Mrs. Harris?"

"That's me. You're probably Shayne?" She put out her hand and looked him over frankly; he seemed to pass. "I was just talking to Rose on the phone. Some excitement you had out there this morning, and I wish you'd tell me what the hell it was all about."

"Can I take you somewhere?"

"No, let's go inside, o.k.? I was on my way over to that pipsqueak Painter. I have a piece of information for him, and this time there better not be any crap about not letting me in."

She unlocked the door. They started up the stairs, which were too narrow to walk on side by side. Shayne was several steps behind. She was wearing a tight black skirt and very high heels, and Shayne had no trouble observing that she was trimly built.

She looked back at him. "Finding your way all right? Somebody's going to kill himself on these stairs some day. Don't lean on the banisters. I'd hate to lose you at this stage of the game."

Shayne laughed. After four flights, she took him along a

narrow hall and unlocked a door which let them into a small, almost airless apartment. Shayne got a better look at her as she took his hat. Her make-up was slightly excessive, but it had been put on carefully. Her figure was as good from the front as from the back. She had a small, stubborn mouth and hard eyes.

"Can I give you something?" she said. "All I've got in the way of liquor is gin, and I'm not going to offer you any of that because I want you to keep sharp. The time factor is terrific. The way you look, you could use some coffee."

"Sure, if it's no trouble."

"Hell, I don't have time for anything that's trouble."

She had a two-burner unit on a counter in a little alcove which could possibly be called a kitchen. She put on water to boil and spooned out instant coffee into two cups.

"What's the matter with that little two-bit Hitler over on the Beach, anyway?" she demanded. "He solved a case once. Great. Everybody probably told him he was a marvellous detective, and he felt very respected. So now he's got a vested interest. I tell him, solve the goddam case all over again. Prove Sam is innocent after all, and he'll get tremendous publicity. He convicted a guy, but his conscience wouldn't let him rest, and so on. They'd write editorials about it. A thing like that could only happen in America—you know how it goes. But he won't listen to a word out of me any more, and the calendar is crowding us. Sit down, Mr. Shayne. This takes about a minute and a half."

Shayne picked up a straight chair and turned it backward. "Maybe he already has a new solution, and he's just holding it up so he can break it with a real splash."

"What?" she said sharply. "How do you mean, a real splash? What's he waiting for, the last half-hour countdown?"

"I don't think even Petey would go that far. But he wouldn't mind holding up a day or two, even a week or two, if he saw a chance to come out of it with bigger space in the papers."

"Then it's simple," she said decisively. "Let's get the newspaper boys together and blast him."

"I like your approach, Mrs. Harris," Shayne said, grinning, "but first let's get something to blast him with. What's this piece of information you're taking to him?"

"I found out where Milburn is."

"Who?"

"Fred Milburn. That won't mean anything to you, I guess. How much did Rose tell you?"

"She said something about a letter."

"Yeah—that's how this started. Have you got a cigarette you can give me?"

Shayne fished one out for her and offered his lighter. She took a deep drag and breathed out smoke.

"Come on, damn you, boil," she said, talking to the water on the burner. "Everything takes so damn long lately! I've been as nervous as a flea for the last month or so, and it seems to get worse. Here's how it happened. I wanted something to take my mind off, and I was cleaning out some old trunks and junk, and I found this letter. You know about Sam's defense? He said he couldn't have robbed the damn bank because he was somewhere else that night. They asked him where. He said with me. Well, he wasn't with me, and never mind how they proved *that*, but they proved it. This was all Painter's doing, and it gave him a fixed idea about my morals, or lack of morals. You're following this, I trust."

The water came to a boil, and she filled the cups. She gave Shayne one and sat down across the table. "There's cream and sugar, if you want it, or maybe there is."

"Black's fine," Shayne said.

"He made a pass at me at the time, I might add. I nearly chewed off his arm."

"*Painter?*" Shayne said incredulously.

"He thought he'd found something available. I wasn't *that* available, thank God, but it may explain this high-and-mighty-and-don't-bother-me act of his lately. Where was I?

Well, after his brilliant police work proved that Sam wasn't with me that night, Sam said he'd tell the truth. He was sticking up a gas station in Alabama, with another guy. A great law-abiding citizen I'm married to, but such is life. They stuck up a few other stores and hit a small payroll, and that's where the twenty thousand came from, that they found in his suitcase.

"I didn't exactly believe him, myself. Somebody actually did stick up that gas station, though, and they took Sam up for an identification. Well, you know eye-witnesses. When you want them, they're half blind in one eye and all-blind in the other. When you don't want them, they've got twenty-twenty vision and a wonderful imagination. And this gas-station guy in Alabama said he'd never set eyes on Sam in his life. That kind of did it, as far as I was concerned."

"Were you on good terms with him at the time?"

"Why shouldn't I be? He played around, I played around, but we had a very good marriage, what there was of it. They were always busting him for something, and I didn't exactly go into holy orders every time they turned the key on him for a few years. So I said to him, Sam, if you're going to insist on that alibi, who were you robbing *with*? Because produce him, I said, let's see what he has to say. But he wouldn't. He said the guy had two felonies already, and the next time was for keeps. Well, it was his own fault, I said, if he went out sticking up places with a habitual hanging over his head, but Sam wouldn't see it that way. Now nobody's that public-spirited, I mean with the rap Sam was up against himself, and I made up my mind it was all talk, he wanted to cop a plea to armed robbery and get out of murder. Except it didn't work."

"How much did he pay the lawyer?"

"The court allowed something out of that twenty thousand, not a hell of a lot. All right. This letter. If you want to know the truth, I'd been through those trunks before, looking for something that might show where he'd stashed away all that extra dough, granted he actually robbed the Beach Trust, which I thought he had. Who am I to disagree with a jury? I didn't find anything. This time I was going to give it one more run-through before I called the junk man to pick it up.

"And I found a letter signed Fred, all folded and rumpled up. I don't even know why he happened to keep it, just one of those accidents. I know the damn thing by heart. Fred, whoever *he* was, said he'd meet Sam in such-and-such a hotel in Mobile, and not to chicken out because he had a couple of girls lined up. Then there was some more nothing stuff—he ran into so-and-so the other day, he wanted to send regards, you can see why I skipped over it the first time. The big point was, the date. It was dated three days before the bank bust, and it said for Sam to be in Mobile *three days later*.

"But there was no year on it, just the month and the day, and it could have been some different year, for all I knew. But it was the first thing gave me the idea he might be telling the truth. The next time I was visiting him, I threw in some innocent little question, like did Fred ever get in touch with him? He said who, Fred Milburn? And then he shut up fast. I asked around about Fred Milburn, and it turned out he actually had two felony convictions going against him, so that part of it fits."

"Is he a local man?" Shayne said.

"From South Carolina, but he doesn't stay put. I went up to that Mobile hotel and paid five bucks to look at the register for that day. Nothing. Naturally the boys wouldn't use their right names, but I couldn't see any handwriting that looked like my Sam's. Of course I'm no expert, and Sam never wrote me many letters. What I had to do was find Milburn and turn him in, so the cops could try him on those old stick-ups. I know it's kind of cold by now, but I thought maybe Milburn had caught that habitual and he wouldn't have anything to lose.

"So that's what I took to Painter, the letter and the name. You'd think a cop could take it from there, because somebody with that many convictions, the cops tend to keep track of where he is and what he's doing. And I practically had to beat Painter over the head before he'd touch it. What's wrong with the guy? I gave him a week, and went back to see what he'd found out, if anything. He put me in the revolving door and revolved me right out. Grim. I came back the next day and the day after that and the day after *that*. They're getting sick of me there in the upper brackets. The boys on the desk don't mind. We kid around."

"What made you think of Mrs. Heminway?"

"She's a doll, isn't she? Well, the lawyer said he couldn't do a thing through the courts without more to go on, and I was wondering how I could light a fire under Painter. I kept seeing her name in the paper, raising money for charity or something. I could use a little charity myself. We were pretty much in the same boat. She lost her husband. I lost mine. She and her poppa are the kind of taxpayers who can put the screws on a public servant and get a little action, or that's what I thought. We had a good cry together, and she said she'd try. She landed on Painter like a ton of bricks, and to my great surprise, he gave her the same run-around he gave me. So what's the point in being rich?"

"Can you think of any reason why somebody would want to shoot her?"

"God, Mr. Shayne, it really beats me." A troubled look came into her eyes, the first sign of uncertainty Shayne had seen her show. "When she was just a name in the paper I thought I could use her to hit Painter with, and why not? The widow and the widow-to-be, it made a terrific combination, and I still don't know why it didn't work. But I don't want anything to happen to her on my account. I don't know how to say it. She's terrific, that's all.

"And don't let that way of hers fool you. She wouldn't pass out free samples, but if she liked somebody she'd be sexy as hell, you can take my word for it. Don't get me wrong, that's a compliment. She's *human*. I thought at first Fred Milburn must be mixed up in this thing this morning, but what kind of sense—? No, the thing is, the dough. If Sam didn't pull the Beach Trust job, whoever did sure as hell didn't pay any taxes on it."

Shayne looked down into his coffee cup. There was nothing left but the dregs. He swirled them around, but they didn't fall into any recognizable pattern.

"I'm going to ask you a touchy question, Mrs. Harris."

"You might as well call me Norma," she said, breaking in, "especially if you're going to start asking touchy questions."

"Okay, Norma. What's your main interest here, your husband or the money?"

She laughed. "You think that's going to hurt my feelings? I can be interested in more than one thing at a time. If Sam did it and I can get a postponement, that gives me more time to worm out of him where he put it. And if somebody else did, maybe I can get him off and beat the cops to the dough. Why not? That's why I got so enthusiastic when Rosie suggested hiring you. I know your reputation—and don't *you* get your feelings hurt.

"But the story I hear on you is that when something extra comes your way, you don't hand it over to the Salvation Army. I'm not thinking of the full amount, you understand. I'm a dreamer, but I don't dream in Cinemascope. I know I couldn't get away with it. I'm thinking about the percentage from the insurance company, and what I was going to suggest —if you get that percentage on the strength of information I give you, wouldn't half the recovery fee be about right?"

She said quickly as Shayne frowned, "Which doesn't mean I want Sam to get the chair. I've got the kind of mind that can think ahead. If Sam's broke when he gets out, he's just going robbing again."

Shayne gave a short laugh. "Twenty-five percent would be generous. And if I get Sam off, which looks pretty doubtful at the moment, I'll give it to him, not you. You won't mind so long as it's in the family."

"You bastard," she said. "A third?"

"A quarter. And I hope you realize we're cutting up a percentage of something that may not exist."

"Maybe, but I've got a feeling. If anybody can do it, you can."

She stood up, smoothing her skirt down over her well-rounded hips, and came around the table. She touched Shayne's cheek. Bending down, she kissed him on the mouth.

"You're a nice-looking guy, Mike," she said, "and I hope I can talk you into giving that thirty-three and a third percent to me and not to Sam. He's not very good with money. He'd just throw it away."

"Twenty-five," Shayne said.

Straightening, she let one breast graze his face. "Hell, twenty-five. And that doesn't mean I'm not thinking of Sam. It's mixed up together, and I think maybe you're one of the few people who might be able to understand it. Now you've got my mind running along the wrong lines."

"All I've done is sit here and drink coffee," Shayne said.

"Yeah. All you've done is sit there drinking coffee with pants on. How many men do you think I've had up here to give coffee to in the last three years?"

"You don't want me to answer that, Norma."

"No, I guess I don't. I'd be insulted no matter what you said. I wish we had the time to give this more attention, but if we're going to make any money, you've got to get out of here."

She went back to her own side of the table. "I found Fred Milburn. And why that comic-opera gumshoe Painter couldn't find him two weeks ago is something I'd like to have somebody explain to me. I called up everybody I could think of, and asked if they knew what had happened to good old Fred Milburn, because I had something I thought would interest him. Nobody did, but I told them to contact me if they heard anything, and this morning one of them did. He's in the slammer. If it wasn't serious, it'd be funny. He picked up a dozen parking tickets over a couple of years, and he threw them in the wastebasket. He's doing thirty days hard labor, and that's where you'll find him, in the county jail. But this is the twenty-ninth day, so as much as I hate to say it, you'd better get moving."

"In a minute," Shayne said thoughtfully. "Do you know if Painter checked on that Mobile hotel? There must be pictures of Milburn he could use. Or did he put out a flier?"

"As far as I know he didn't do a damn thing but sit on his butt, if you'll pardon the expression."

"Now don't be jumpy, Norma. If Milburn's in jail he won't run away before I get there. Your lawyer's cockeyed—he doesn't need any more facts than you've given me to get Sam a postponement. If he drags his heels we'll get another lawyer. The town's full of lawyers who'd handle it for the publicity. But that's just half of it. You've been thinking about this a lot longer than I have. If Sam didn't rob the bank, who did?"

"I've been thinking about it, all right," Norma said. "I keep asking myself questions, like why did George Heminway pick that one night to work late? Things like that happen, God knows, but maybe it wasn't an accident, huh? In my experience, who goes into a bank these days without somebody inside steering them? The way the alarm was knocked out—I know damn well Sam didn't do that. Other times he always paid an electrician good money to take care of the wiring. Well, you're the Professor. You figure it out."

"Have you run into Rose's father?"

"Just to say hello to. He was itching to ask the butler to show me out, not that they have a butler. But he didn't like his daughter to get mixed up with unsavory characters." She laughed without rancor. "Rose said he practically tore up the scenery after I left."

"Does Baltimore mean anything to you? Did Sam ever pull any jobs that far north?"

"No, he always stayed south of the Mason-Dixon line. He's got an accent you can cut with a knife, and he was afraid it made him stick out."

"Did he ever belong to the Truckers Union?"

"What's that got to do with anything? Hell, no—Sam's strong against unions. He thinks a good man can always get ahead on his own. I know he picked a funny way to prove it, but that's how he is."

"Do you know if he ever borrowed money from a shark on the Beach named Sticky Horvath?"

"I doubt it. If he did he never told me."

He thought for another moment. "Norma, what were you doing last night? Where were you between eight and nine?"

"Right here," she said promptly. "All by my lonesome." When he looked at her skeptically she said, "Well, I was. And what was happening between eight and nine other places?"

"I'm trying to find that out."

"Okay, *be* mysterious. What do I do now, Mike, go to Painter with this or not?"

He stood up. "Better not."

"I didn't think so." She came to the door with him. "I want to keep this from Sam as long as I can. I mean that I'm the one who found Milburn. It may be hard to believe, but I really think he'd let them turn on the juice before he gave them anybody's name. I'm not in that league myself, but maybe it's not such a bad way to be. And finally, can you loan me fifty bucks?"

Shayne snorted. He took a ten out of his wallet and gave it to her. "Be thinking about that Truckers' connection. Maybe something will come to you."

10

MICHAEL SHAYNE ANGRILY ground out his cigarette in the nearest ashtray, which was already overflowing. Three of the butts were his. He was wasting too much time. He threw aside the ancient copy of *Life*, the only magazine in the waiting room, uncrossed his long legs and stood up. The secretary at the desk near the door, a gray-haired woman with a masculine haircut and severe horn-rimmed glasses, continued to type as he approached.

"In confidence," Shayne said, "is the warden really busy, or is this to make me realize what a big man he is?"

The secretary's fingers lifted from the keys, and the corner of her mouth moved. "In confidence, Mr. Shayne, I only work here."

"I'd forgotten how hard it is to get into jail when you want to get in."

A buzzer sounded. "That may be for you, Mr. Shayne. Excuse me."

She opened the door to the warden's office and looked in, then opened it all the way. "You may go in now."

Shayne gave her a half-wink as he passed. The warden looked up from an open folder, but he didn't get out of his swivel chair or offer to shake hands. He was a plump man in glasses, and looked like an insurance salesman who hasn't ever succeeded in selling much insurance.

"So you're interested in one of my thirty-day men, are you?" he snapped. "Why?"

Shayne sat down without being asked to do so. "I've been retained to investigate a series of small stick-ups a few years ago in southern Alabama, among other things. I have information that Milburn may be involved."

"You're no novice, Shayne. You surely must know that there isn't a prison warden in the country who would turn over one of his prisoners for questioning in a police matter. What's your real angle?"

Shayne said carefully, "I understand his thirty days are about up. I'd like to find out exactly when you're letting him out, so I won't miss him. I had a hard time finding him, and I don't want him to disappear again."

"He won't disappear." He tapped on the desk with the sharp end of a pencil, reversed it and tapped with the eraser. "We're through with him here at noon tomorrow. But you can save yourself a trip. I've got a hold-order on him. He's being called for."

Shayne relaxed visibly. "That's fine. Sooner or later the law of averages catches up with everybody, even Petey Painter, and he does something right. That's who's picking him up?"

The warden looked at that question from all angles before deciding to answer. "I think it's in order for me to give out that information. We're turning the man over on an armed robbery warrant."

"I wasn't sure Petey was that up to date. Did he just have the one session with him?"

The warden threw down his pencil and looked at Shayne from beneath lowered brows. "What is this, a fishing expedition, by any chance?"

The redhead grinned. "You might call it that. You know Lieutenant Wing, don't you?"

"Sure, I know Joe Wing. Why?"

"I didn't think you'd make a prisoner available unless I had a cop with me, so I asked Wing to meet me here. You kept me waiting so long he ought to be showing up any minute. He'll be in a hurry. Could you get Milburn down in the visitors' room so we won't have any more delays?"

"Dear God!" the warden exclaimed. "You'd think I had nothing else to do but run errands for the Miami Beach police. Milburn's working. He owes the county one more day of hard labor. He'll be delighted to talk to you boys about something that happened a few years ago. Just delighted. He'll talk to you steadily all day, till he hears the five o'clock quitting whistle. A hell of a way to run a jail, is all I have to say." He stabbed a button on his desk, and when his secretary put her head in again he said, "Fred Milburn. They can probably find him in the chair shop. Have him brought to Interrogation."

"Yes, sir. Lieutenant Wing is waiting."

"Send him in."

The warden not only stood up for Wing, he shook hands. Wing shot Shayne a glance. The redhead said, "Did Petey say anything about getting out a warrant for somebody named Fred Milburn?"

"Not to me," Wing said.

"It's only verbal so far," the warden said. "He didn't want to go through all the rigamarole out of writing up a transfer. I gave him the release date, so he could make the arrest as the guy walked out. Sit down. What are you up to, Joe, if it's not too inquisitive? I never thought I'd see the day when Painter's lieutenants were going around checking up on him."

Wing sat down around the corner from Shayne. "We seem to be setting precedents right and left. The fact is—well, we can't keep it corked very much longer—the son of a bitch has disappeared."

The warden stared. "*Painter?*"

"And let's keep that between these four stone walls for the time being," Wing said. "I still hope he'll be at his desk when I get back, raising hell as usual. I hate to think of those headlines."

"But disappeared?" the warden said. "He's probably just gone underground. He was being very cloak-and-dagger when he was out here. I just about had to swear a blood oath before he'd even tell me who he wanted to see. A great man for that kind of stuff."

"Could be," Wing said. "And if he's just off somewhere pretending to be Sherlock Holmes, he won't like this a damn bit. But I'd look pretty dumb if there's something serious wrong and I just sit back and manicure my fingernails, because I'm scared he'll bawl me out."

The warden's eyes glinted. "I don't care for Painter any more than the next man, but we don't want anything serious to happen to him, do we?" He gave a surprising hoot of laughter, which made him seem more human. "I'll be goddammed."

"And this is in confidence, right?"

"Absolutely," the warden said heartily, but without convincing Shayne. Tim Rourke had probably ferreted out the story by this time anyway. The warden went on, "But when I think of how he ordered my secretary out and just about looked under the rug to be sure I hadn't planted some pixie there to spy on him—"

"Did he bring a driver?" Shayne said.

"Now that you mention it, he didn't. He came in a taxi. The city probably paid for it, but still."

"He was only here once?" Wing said.

The warden nodded. "My secretary might remember what day it was, if it's important. Last week some time. If he didn't want people to notice him, he certainly didn't succeed. He played hell with our routine. The men were eating their dinner, and of course Mr. Bigshot couldn't wait till they were finished, so we could bring Milburn in without making a special thing of it. We had to haul him out of the mess-hall, and everybody watched him go. He's got a habitual rap coming to him next, and you know that old prison superstition, that two-time losers are good pigeon material because they have more at stake."

"It's more than a superstition," Shayne said.

"That may be. We've been having some trouble about the chow lately—the papers haven't got hold of it, thank God. Taking Milburn out of the mess-hall set off a little racket. Nothing serious, a little rattling of cups and silverware. It quieted down after we grabbed a few of the ringleaders, guys we've had our eye on for quite some time. The point I'm making, I didn't have time to chaperone Painter. I left him with Milburn, and then I had my hands full. I guess he got what he came for, because when I saw him again he was beaming. He looked like the cat who swallowed—what was it, a canary?"

"You know Painter. He made arrangements for picking up Milburn on his release date, and delivered some uncalled-for remarks about what would happen to me if I discharged the prisoner before Painter arrived to make the arrest. I've been in this business a long time, and nothing like that has ever happened, or ever will happen. So Painter's in trouble, is he?" He smiled broadly. "Well, well. Excuse me. I'm laughing on the outside and crying on the inside."

"Painter was beaming," Shayne said. "What was the prisoner doing?"

"Hell, Shayne—I don't have my people long enough so I can tell anything by how they look. And Painter was holding forth. I didn't give Milburn any serious study."

The door opened abruptly. Looking around, Shayne saw the secretary and a uniformed guard. The guard beckoned the warden outside with a quick twist of the head. The warden got up hurriedly. Shayne and Wing were right behind him.

"Real trouble this time," the guard said.

Whirling, he set off at a half run. The others pounded after him. At the end of the corridor, they ran through a barred door that was standing open. At the next barred door the warden flung over his shoulder, "Not you, Shayne. Wait here."

Shayne decided that he hadn't heard him. The warden was in too much of a hurry to stop and make it stick.

They entered a busy shop. At long benches along one end of the room, a number of men wearing faded blue work clothes, with serial numbers stencilled above their breast pockets, were weaving cane seats for finished chairs. They seemed deeply absorbed in their work, so preoccupied with making the pattern come out right that they didn't notice the warden's party. At the lathes and drill-presses, other inmates were turning chair-legs and drilling holes for rungs, with the same seriousness and attention to detail.

The guard, walking rapidly, led the way between two long rows of busy lathes. There was a pleasant smell of sawdust and wood-chips. None of the prisoners looked around. They were as tense as if they had been shooting craps for large stakes. The guard stopped.

One of the workers had slumped against his machine. His head rested in a litter of chips and machine-oil. A chair-leg, mounted between centers, continued to revolve at high speed.

The warden pulled at his shoulder, and he came all the way back, his head rolling. The warden caught him under both arms. The front of his work clothes was soaked with blood, and the handle of one of the turning chisels protruded from his stomach beneath his breastbone. He was alive, but he was breathing harshly and desperately, and Shayne didn't think he could live much longer.

11

NO ONE HAD to identify this man for Shayne. The redhead knew it had to be Fred Milburn. He died on the oily floor before the prison doctor could reach him. He was a small, nondescript-appearing man, with a slight build, a thin face and what in life had probably been an unassuming manner. No doubt his manner changed when he had a gun in his hand.

One of the guards pulled a master switch cutting off the power to the machines. Another ordered the men to come to attention beside their benches. They stood up, one by one, without hurrying. They didn't look at the guards or the dead man, and in fact didn't appear to be looking at anything at all. Shayne recognized one or two, but they had pulled back behind an invisible curtain.

A bell clanged, and the prisoners turned at another command and walked off in single file. The warden frowned when he noticed Shayne.

"Goddammit, did I give you permission to come in here? This is great, just great. Nobody pays any attention to what I say in this place."

The redhead stared down at Milburn, his eyes hooded. After a second he met the warden's look.

"Fine. I've got other things to do."

He started to turn, but the warden made a quick movement. "Oh, no, you don't. You barged in here and asked to see one of my people, and before the message could get to him, he was stabbed. Now you think you can walk out without answering any questions? And tell your friends on the newspapers what happened? No, sir. It won't be as easy to get out as it was to get in."

Shayne exchanged a look with Lieutenant Wing.

Wing said, "I'm out of my jurisdiction, Mike. Somebody else is going to be asking the questions."

"And you're going to be answering them, too," the warden told Shayne. "Believe me! This is no goddam joke." He took out a handkerchief and mopped his forehead. "Well, let's break the news to the sheriff."

The dead man was left lying where he was until the sheriff arrived with two carloads of helpers. Shayne was taken back to the waiting room outside the warden's office. There he finished his pack of cigarettes, listened to the clacking of the secretary's typewriter, and went back patiently over everything he had been told by Norma Harris and Rose Heminway. The lines on his face were deeply etched.

The sheriff was a pleasant fat man named Woodrow Wilson Smith, with a politician's smile which he showed Shayne briefly as he came into the waiting room with the warden and a small crowd of assistants.

"Might as well come in, Mike," he said. "We're going to be using the warden's office. I know you don't want to hang around any longer than you have to."

He waved Shayne to the chair he had occupied earlier. He himself took the warden's chair, and one of the young men with him opened a notebook. The sheriff gave the redhead another friendly smile, apparently not seeing a man but a potential vote.

"I won't start firing questions at you, Mike," he said. "You and I have always got along fine, and I hope we can keep it that way. Why don't you just tell me in your own words how you happened to want to talk to this fellow Milburn, and then we'll take it from there."

Shayne went over what was now familiar ground, and the young man wrote it down in shorthand. At the end, the sheriff rewarded him with a smile that was even more brilliant than the one he normally wore.

"I like the way you organize things, Mike," he said. "I wish more people had that gift. A few small points. When Chief Painter was here last week, if Milburn admitted that he and Sam Harris were mixed up in shenanigans up in Alabama the night of the big bank job, well, that's a terrific piece of news, front-page stuff. Painter's no recluse, as far as publicity's concerned. Why didn't he spring it right away?"

Shayne spread his hands. "I gave up trying to follow Petey's reasoning about ten minutes after I met him."

"You don't think there's a chance he found out something different? Milburn and Harris were friends. Maybe they were working together on the big one. I always did think it was screwy, one man handling something that size. And then the dough." His smile disappeared and he leaned forward. "Mrs. Sam Harris found Milburn for you. I don't like to cast reflections on any lady, but it seems to me she might be thinking more about what happened to that good bread than about what's going to happen to her husband. So this occurred to me when you were talking, Mike. Maybe she wanted you to lean on Milburn a little, so he'd cut her a slice?"

"There's nothing to that, Woody," Shayne said, without showing the irritation he felt. "I wouldn't be seeing Milburn alone. Joe Wing was going to be with me."

He was silent while Sheriff Smith studied him, working his lips in and out. The sheriff said, "Now don't take offense at this, Mike, because as far as I know now we're all working the same side of the street. But Joe Wing and myself, we've been talking this over, and I think we're in agreement. We think you're telling the truth as far as you go. But we both have a sneaking suspicion that you don't go quite far enough."

Shayne looked around at the Beach lieutenant, who said, "A couple of things don't add up, Mike."

The sheriff went on, "The warden here makes a suggestion that's a little emotional, but it does express one point of view.

He thinks we ought to put you in the hole on bread and water and see if we can brainwash you. He doesn't mean that literally, but I'm vetoing the whole approach. I wouldn't say that brainwashing Mike Shayne would be one of the easiest jobs in the world. You're going your own way, regardless, and let's hope it turns out all right in the end. But I want to say a couple of things."

"Only a couple, Sheriff?" Shayne said, his eyes narrowing.

"Only a couple, and I think Joe will go along with both of them." He touched his index finger. "The dough. A recovery fee from the insurance company is legitimate loot, and if regular police officers like us aren't allowed to collect, that's our hard luck. But don't try to hold onto more than the legitimate fee, Mike, or we'll make some real trouble for you. Point two is Painter.

"You've got a grievance there, and I'm not the one to say that it's not justified. When it was just between the two of you, the rest of us could sit back and enjoy it. But this thing makes a difference. A guy has been killed. If he was actually dumb enough to go robbing with Sam Harris he was due to spend the rest of his natural life in the can. But he was a human being just the same, and somebody murdered him."

"I appreciate that," Shayne said crisply. "What were you going to say about Painter?"

"Just don't let your feelings lead you astray. That's all. You can go now if you want to. We're going to check back to the Sam Harris defense and get the details on those Alabama stickups. And we're going to be working on the stabbing. We'll take these guys one at a time and hammer them. Between you and me I doubt if we get anything, but we've got to try it. That's what we'll be doing." He looked at Shayne sleepily. "What will you be doing, Mike?"

Shayne smiled. "I'll be making some phone calls."

"That's logical. Who are you going to be making these phone calls to?"

"My client, for one. After that I'm not sure. But I'll check in with you or Wing if I find anything."

The sheriff started to speak, but he made a disgusted gesture and sat back. "You'd better go now, Mike, before I'm tempted to go back to the warden's suggestion. Check in promptly. There's going to be some strong heat on this, and we don't want to learn about something when we see it in the papers."

"You'll be the first to know," Shayne said, standing up. He asked Wing, "Where are you going to be, Joe?"

"Out here, for the time being. I'll leave word where I go. And I want to second what Woody just said. If Milburn passed any information along to Painter, and it looks as though he did, that makes Painter just as hot. We don't want to find *him* with a knife in him."

"Let's look on the bright side," Shayne said. "Maybe they'll use a gun."

"Now Mike," Wing said uneasily.

Shayne's grin disappeared as he went out through the waiting room. Outside, he stopped on the front steps of the forbidding building, his eyes cold and deadly. This made twice. His unknown adversary had failed with Rose Heminway and succeeded with Milburn. Shayne promised himself that there wouldn't be a third time.

He drove carefully, making sure that nobody assigned to him by Sheriff Smith was on his tail. Coming into downtown Miami, he found a parking place, ate a hasty sandwich at a drugstore, bought cigarettes, changed a dollar into dimes and shut himself up in an outdoor phone booth. He tried Rose Heminway's number first. There was no answer. He dialed the other number she had given him—the nursing home. He asked if Mrs. Heminway was there visiting her father.

"I think I saw her come in, sir," a pleasant voice told him. "I'll ring the floor nurse."

He repeated his question to another voice—less pleasant, as nurse's voices are likely to be—and a moment later Rose was on the line.

"Mike! I didn't want to leave the house before you called, but Father gets nervous if I'm not on time."

"How is he?"

"Just the same. But one of these days I know he's going to say hello when I walk in. He keeps trying."

"Is there a place there where we can talk?" Shayne said. "I want to go over a few things."

"I'm sure we can find a place, Mike. If there's anybody in the waiting room we can go outside."

Shayne told her to expect him in half an hour. He spilled a handful of dimes on the shelf, opened a little black book and began to dial. The day bartender of a Miami Beach bar answered. Shayne gave his name and asked several questions. He hung up and tried another number. In the next ten minutes, he used up his dimes and went back into the drugstore to change another dollar.

In Shayne's early years as a detective, when he could work on several cases at once, getting up early, driving hard all day, never going to bed till the bars were closed, he had picked up a wide acquaintance in that twilight world where people live by their brains and their connections, working desperately hard at not working in the ordinary daytime sense. Gamblers, promoters, finders, ten-percenters, they looked on a nine-to-five job with as much distaste as a stretch in jail. The two things they had in common was that they needed money and they kept up with the news that doesn't get in the newspapers. They spent most of their waking hours in public places, their ears open.

Many were still friends of Shayne, though he no longer saw much of them since he started spending evenings with Lucy Hamilton, and many owed him small favors. He had no power or control over them, as cops usually have over their stool pigeons, and there were only two reasons why they gave him information—they liked him, and if it was useful to him he paid well for it.

His fifteenth or sixteenth call was to a man named Kinky Kincaid, a stag-party talent agent. The ringing of the phone interrupted Kinky's afternoon nap in a three-dollar-a-day hotel. He had trouble understanding who was on the line.

"Spain?" he said blurrily. "*Shayne*. Mike, how are you, boy? If this is a business call, I hope I can help you because I'd like to get my wrist-watch out of hock. What time is it, anyway?"

Shayne told him. He said more alertly, "You want to know about Painter?"

"Damn right," Shayne said, surprised. "Do you have anything?"

"I'm so broke these days I can't even buy my own paper, but I read about it over somebody's shoulder and I said to myself, 'Uh-oh.'"

"Why did you say that, Kinky?" Shayne said patiently.

"Wait till I get a cigarette. I'm hung-over from here all the way to Key West. Where are you, Mike? Maybe you could give me a piggy-back ride to the neighborhood saloon and buy me some medicine."

"Sorry, Kinky. I've got a date at the other end of town. I have to do this by phone. Get your cigarette."

A moment later Kincaid's voice continued, "That's better. It's still not good. You're really interested in what happened to the bum? I didn't think you cared."

"I'm on a case," Shayne said briefly. "It seems they're connected."

"He never gave me no personal trouble, but when a cop gets in a jam it gives me a warm feeling inside, like I just had my first shot of the day, you know how it is, Mike?"

"I know just exactly how it is. Where is he, Kinky?"

"Did I say I know where he is? I'm not that kind of source, Mike, and you know it better than I do. I give you these little items, and you put them together with the other little items you get from other people, and you end up with a big fee and your name in the papers, and more power to you. Only this time maybe my item's not so little. I was debating about taking it to the cops, and then I thought what did they ever do for me?"

"Kinky," Shayne said. "Just give me the news."

"Okay, sure. I was on the Beach last night. I don't know when, in the neighborhood of nine but I can't be sure because

"I had to raise some quick dough and I'm without a timepiece at the moment. I was trying to promote a party later on in the week with some Midwest guys I happen to know. And here's where the thing comes in. I know these guys, whenever they're in town they look me up, and it seems funny they didn't get in touch with me before. Too busy, maybe? They're at the St. A. this time, and I see them in the lobby."

"The St. Albans?" Shayne said quickly.

"Nothing but the best. Big Jack Klipstone and Mac something, I don't know his last name, and they're with two others. But they've got no time for their old contact Kincaid. Strictly. Every other time they've been in town, they always had plenty of time for me and the broads. They tell me 'Later, later,' and they walk past like big business men on the way to a board meeting."

"Yeah?" Shayne said when he paused.

"Just taking a drag. What would you do in my shoes, Mike? I always like to know about these things because you never know when they might come in handy. I fake a quarterback sneak for the elevators, but I drift out the side door instead and I get around front in a hurry. I see my party of four get in a new Drive-Urself Chevy and head north. I get in my own Chevy, twelve years old, and *I* head north. After a while they park out in motel country. I park. And I'm very, very careful, Mike, I don't have to tell *you*, because these guys I don't want to know I'm up to any monkey business. The minutes go slow because I'm so nervous. My stomach starts to ache.

"I'm beginning to think this wasn't a hell of a good idea and I ought to stick to my own racket when one of those big police department Caddies comes up Collins like a bat out of hell, the siren on full blast, nearly busted my ear drums. When I say it was going fast, Mike, I mean fast. I didn't get much of a look at who was driving. He didn't have no hat on, and he was kind of low in the seat, but it wouldn't surprise me one damn bit if it was your friend and mine, Peter Painter."

Shayne absently put a cigarette in his mouth. "What about the Chevy?"

"They took off after him, Mike, the four of them. They were running some chances, too, getting off from a standing start that way. They really goosed that buggy. They were over the double line half the time, and where they went from there I don't know. This was too rich for my blood. My Chevy was outclassed, even if I wanted to get into competition, which I didn't. So I came home. Is this worth anything?"

"Seventy-five bucks," Shayne said promptly.

"Hey!" Kincaid said. "Where are you, Mike? I'll come over on my hands and knees and pick it up in my teeth."

"Stay where you are, I'll send it over. That name was Jack Klipstone? And Mac something? What are they doing at the St. Albans? Are they delegates to the Truckers convention?"

"Not exactly delegates, Mike. They're part of Harry Plato's circus.

"Are you sure of that, Kinky?" Shayne said sharply. "They work directly for Plato?"

"You won't quote me, I hope, I hope," Kincaid said, suddenly cautious. "The other two I never saw before, but the word is that there's a lot of beef in town because there's some kind of hassle in the union, and that's what they looked like. Hard boys."

"You said from the Midwest. Where in the Midwest?"

"St. Louis, maybe? I never ask that type too many questions because they might think I'm trying to get personal."

"This helps, Kinky. I've got a few questions about something else, and maybe you can pick up some more change. Put your mind back to the big bank job three years ago, the one they're executing Sam Harris for. I wish I knew what happened to the take. That was a big score, according to all the publicity, but not much of it was found. Did any gossip about that come your way?"

Kincaid thought a moment. "I remember the guys were saying it looked like a stand-in. But it's stale by now. You couldn't prove it by me."

"You mean set up from the inside?"

"You know, Mike—where the inside man guarantees no

trouble and takes the large end of the cut. I do remember we thought it was kind of fantastic that there wasn't any hints around about who maybe did it. I don't mean who actually, who maybe. Usually you run into all kinds of rumors, and the conclusion we came to was that this wasn't a pro job at all, but some do-it-yourself guy with ambitions. Then they picked up Sam Harris, who didn't go with that picture."

"There wasn't any mention of somebody named Fred Milburn?"

"Milburn?" Kincaid said, puzzled. "The one Milburn I know is very smalltime. A delicatessen man. He wouldn't be robbing no banks."

"Did he ever do any work for the Truckers?"

"I don't follow, Mike. The guy's an ordinary heister, in and out. I think I did hear, though, that he did a few stick-ups with Sam Harris. Are you trying to tell me that Painter and that carload of goons last night and a bank job three years ago are part of one and the same thing? Harry Plato's no angel, and that's putting it mildly, but he's got sense enough to steer clear of robbing banks, for God's sake. He makes a pretty good living out of robbing the union." He added hastily, "Don't quote me on that, either."

"Nobody knows I even know you, Kinky, so stop shaking. Think about it, and see what you can turn up. Can you give me a description of the other two guys in the Chevy?"

Kinkaid thought for a moment. "Can't help you there, Mike. Klipstone was the one I was trying to get hold of, and I only got this fast blur of the others. Sports shirts, no ties. But they gave you the impression you wouldn't want to disagree with them because it wouldn't be good for your teeth. I could probably pick them out of a line-up, but you know as well as I do that I'm not going to do any damn-fool thing like that."

"You don't think one of them was a Cuban? Or a husky kid, about a hundred and seventy, thick jowls, thick neck?"

"Sorry, Mike. No cigar."

"You've given me something to think about, Kinky," Shayne said slowly, "and I'll make that a hundred instead of seventy-five. If you go out, leave word where I can reach you."

"I'm sure as hell not going out till I get that hundred."

Shayne laughed and hung up.

12

HE WAITED A MOMENT, thinking, his hand on the phone. It was too soon to ask Joe Wing to walk into the St. Albans ballroom and pick out Klipstone and the others. The identification was too shaky. One big trouble with this kind of information was that the source couldn't be mentioned, if he wanted to go on getting information like it. If asked a direct question by someone in uniform, Kincaid would cheerfully swear on the Bible that he hadn't been near the St. Albans lobby in weeks, and had never set eyes on Jack Klipstone in his life. Shayne still had some work to do before he could pass this on to the cops.

He found a Western Union office, where he put a hundred dollar bill in an envelope, addressed it to Kincaid at his hotel, and paid the messenger fee. Then he drove to the nursing home on the Beach, where he had arranged to meet Rose Heminway.

It was a rambling three-story building inside a tall spiked fence. It looked out over the lower bay, and was reached by a narrow shell road off West Avenue. Squire, the Beach detective who had been assigned to look after Mrs. Heminway, was rocking gently in a glider on the wide porch, half asleep.

He started to his feet as Shayne came up the steps. "Oh, you, Mike," he said. "It's been a long day. Do you think I could go home?"

"Why not ask Wing for relief?"

"What do you think I've been doing? I've been asking for relief all afternoon. But it seems we're on emergency shifts, and if I fall asleep it's just too damn bad."

"Keep your eyes open," Shayne said. "You want to find Painter, don't you?"

"Oh, sure," Squire said dryly.

Hearing voices, Rose came out from inside. She was wearing a simple pink dress with large buttons, and in spite of the dark shadows beneath her eyes, Shayne thought she looked as fresh as if she had just stepped out of a shower. He corrected himself hastily, remembering that morning. For one thing, she had more clothes on.

She put her hand on his arm. "Mike, you're a comfortable sight. Detective Squire has been wonderful, but he's getting a little drowsy. He was up all night, he tells me."

"He's not the only one," Shayne said. Squire was looking at him hopefully, and Shayne said, "I'll see what Wing thinks. I'm going to be with Mrs. Heminway for a while, and there's no point in doubling up."

Rose showed him a phone booth inside, and Shayne called Wing, who grudgingly gave permission for Squire to quit for the day. The detective left in a hurry before they could change their minds.

Rose indicated the glider. "Or we could walk down to the water, Mike."

"Let's walk," Shayne said.

They started down the steps, and Shayne said, "Can your father move in any way? If you asked him a question, could he react enough to say yes or no?"

"Not now," she said hopelessly. "I tried just that, as soon as he was able to move his right arm. But he can't seem to communicate between his brain and his muscles. I'm convinced there's no brain damage, no matter what the doctors say. I think he knows me part of the time. It's terrible to see how he looks at me, as though he's struggling to say something. What did you want to ask him?"

Shayne didn't answer. They were walking down the long lawn toward a sandy beach. "Apparently you didn't have any trouble with the Lüger this morning."

"What do you mean, I didn't have any trouble?" she said

indignantly. "I finally worked myself up to pulling the trigger, and the wretched thing jumped right out of my hand. I mean it, that's exactly what happened. It leaped up and went sailing over my shoulder. I only managed to fire the one shot, but you were right, the man outside was as nervous as I was. He didn't wait to find out what had happened to his friend. The police must have passed him on the causeway. Did you find out where he went?"

"Yeah. I'll get to that in a minute."

"Mike, I thought I'd better say—I've been feeling embarrassed about the way I acted when you climbed in through the window." She touched her face, which had reddened, and looked resolutely out across the water. "I thought you were—I know it was silly, and I don't even know exactly what I'm trying to say now except that I hope you don't think—" She broke off, flushing.

Shayne grinned. "You were very cute, as a matter of fact, and that's enough of that, if we're going to get anything done."

She gave him a sidelong glance. "Yes, Mr. Shayne," she murmured.

They came to a wooden bench at the edge of the grass and sat down.

"Quite a few things have happened since I saw you," Shayne said. He offered her a cigarette and took one himself. "But first I'd like to ask you some questions. Don't try to figure out why I'm asking. Just answer them as they come, and then we'll see how they add up."

His lighter flared between them. "That sounds sensible," she said, breathing out smoke.

"To start with the robbery. Did you or your husband ever have anything to do, at any time, with either Sam Harris or Fred Milburn?"

She shook her head. "I can't be positive about George, but I certainly never heard either name."

"How much was your husband earning at the time he was killed?"

"Fifty-six hundred. Everybody in the bank assumed he was on his way up, being the president's son-in-law. But Father's old-fashioned about things like that. I even think he leaned over backward, so people wouldn't think he was playing favorites. He passed George over for one promotion which he really should have had, in my biased opinion. George had the responsibility, without the money or the title to go with it. I will say that George was too easygoing. He let people walk all over him. *He* didn't care."

"You weren't living with your father then?"

"No, we had our own apartment. Mother was still alive. She was in and out of hospitals the last few years. It was a bad time for all of us."

"Did you and George live within your income?"

"Why do—no, that's right, I'm not supposed to ask any questions. Most of the time we came close, Mike. We had to borrow from Father now and then, but usually we managed to pay it back when we said we would."

"Was your marriage happy?"

"Very," she said quietly.

"He wasn't involved with any other women?"

"Involved! Certainly not." She looked at him directly. "I don't care—I have to ask a question. Are you implying that he had something to do with the robbery?"

"That's what I'm implying. It's not necessarily true. When people are given responsible jobs and not enough pay to make ends meet, they've been known to make ends meet by dipping into the till. I'm not saying that happened, but it would explain a few things."

She smoothed her dress. "Mike—I know strange things happen, but I honestly don't think I could be that wrong about anybody. We were married three years. We were still as much in love as when we were on our honeymoon, and we just didn't have any secrets from each other. We spent our free time together. When could he get mixed up with other women? In the morning coffee break? They didn't even have a coffee-break at the bank. It's physically impossible. I managed our checkbook. I knew what came in and went out, to the penny. On top of all that, I knew George."

"Tell me again why he worked overtime that night."

"There was some kind of department deadline, something was moved up and he was the only one who could handle it. I don't suppose anyone would remember now."

"But it wasn't a regular thing?"

"If it had been, I *would* have suspected he was seeing another woman." Her face clouded. "He was depressed about something, though. It was a rare thing for him to worry. Our finances were pretty tight just then, and the way the hospital bills were piling up, Father didn't have anything to spare. It was probably that. I couldn't get him to cheer up. He went around with a gloomy face on all the time, very snappish and cross, and we had some bad fights. Not about anything, really. He was in such a rotten frame of mind that anything could set him off."

Shayne smoked for a moment in silence. "Did he ever belong to a union?"

"No, he went to work at the bank just after he got out of the service, and there weren't any unions there."

"Do you know the name Harry Plato?"

"The name, but that's all."

Shayne flicked his cigarette into the grass. "Or Luke Quinn? He's an official in the international now, but he used to be head of the Miami local."

"Luke Quinn?" she said thoughtfully. "A serious-looking man?"

Shayne nodded. "About thirty-five. He wears glasses now, and he looks more like a TV announcer than the popular idea of a labor leader."

"I think that's the one. There was some kind of city-wide committee, I think for the Red Cross, with representatives from business and labor and the Kiwanis Club and so on. Father was chairman, and they sometimes met at his house. They divided the city in sections, like a military operation, and Father was very pleased when they raised more money than anybody ever had before."

"Let's jump to the present," Shayne said. "Did your father say anything to you before he went to see Painter?"

"I'm ashamed to say, Mike, that we weren't on very good terms. I don't mean we weren't speaking, but we weren't speaking very cordially. We'd disagreed bitterly when I wanted to help Norma. The day of his stroke he just called a cab and put on his hat and left. He didn't even say where he was going."

Shayne pulled reflectively at his earlobe. "Rose, I know you've been thinking about what happened this morning, and I hope you've come up with something."

She shook her head. "I had a long session with Lieutenant Wing, and we both kept thinking of the most far-fetched possibilities. But nothing helped. The name Cole means nothing to me. Baltimore means nothing to me. It's very creepy, and I've been grateful for having a detective looking after me all day, I assure you. But what's going to *happen*, Mike?"

"There's some kind of deadline," Shayne said. "The obvious one is Sam Harris's execution, but that's not enough. The Truckers are electing officers tomorrow, but I can't see that that means anything. Well, my next stop is the St. Albans, which this week is no place for a lady. I don't want you to go home. I'll put you in an out-of-the-way hotel, and you'd better register under a different name."

She stood up when he did, her face troubled. "Mike, that scares me. I don't like to be all by myself in a hotel."

"Wing will assign you another detective if you ask him," Shayne said. "But bodyguards work both ways. They give you a certain amount of protection, but they also attract attention. It's safer just to drop out of sight. I'll make sure that nobody follows us."

"You know about these things," she said doubtfully, "but I can promise you I won't get any sleep. I'll just look in on Father before we go."

Shayne's eyes were bleak as they went up the sloping lawn. He was doing some hard thinking. Somewhere there had to be a link, and he knew that much depended on how fast he could find it. In a city as large as Miami, he could hide Rose where she would be perfectly safe so long as she followed a few simple directions. He was worrying about Peter Painter. Rose had talked to Painter, and a gunman was sent to call on her. Fred Milburn talked to Painter, and he was knifed.

The longer Shayne thought about it, the worse it looked. And yet the only constructive thing he could think of to do about it was to collect Joe Wing and a few cops and walk in on the leadership of the Truckers. And that was only constructive by comparison with other ideas he'd had. He didn't expect it to get him anywhere. He didn't know what questions to ask. The Trucker officials weren't amateurs; they wouldn't break down at the sight of a badge.

He went inside with Rose. In the front hall she forced a smile and started upstairs. Shayne turned into the waiting room, which had been the living room of the house when it had been a private residence. It was nicely furnished, with comfortable chairs and sofas. Several old people were watching a television program, and in one corner of the room a young doctor was talking to a man and woman, probably relatives of one of his patients. A small adjoining room had been turned into an office, where a young girl was serving a telephone switchboard.

She was saying, "I'm afraid there hasn't been any change. Mrs. Heminway is here now, if you'd care to speak to her."

Shayne listened idly, his attention divided between what she was saying and the loud dialogue from the TV screen. She went on, "That's perfectly all right. I'm just sorry I haven't any better news."

Shayne sauntered over to the doorway as she accepted another incoming call. "Sunset Nursing Home, good evening." She seemed too young to be earning her own living, but girls of that age had a way of looking younger to Shayne each year. She plugged a jack into the board and looked up.

Shayne said, "Doesn't this job get monotonous?"

"Oh, I don't know," she said. "You're—Michael Shayne, aren't you?"

Shayne admitted that was who he was.

"That detective who came with Mrs. Heminway wouldn't talk to me at all," she said. "Is it true"—she lowered her voice and her eyes widened—"that somebody *tried to kill her?*"

"I'm afraid it is," Shayne said.

She shuddered slightly. "I couldn't believe it."

"Does her father get many calls?"

She cheered up. "Oh, all the time, from all over. He must have a terrific circle of friends. It keeps me real busy, not that I mind. I try to say something cheerful, but the doctor doesn't think there's really much chance the paralysis will wear off, after this long. I probably should not say this, but I don't think it matters, do you, I mean to tell somebody like you? Excuse me."

She answered another call and rang an extension.

Shayne said, "When you said he gets calls from all over, you mean long-distance?"

"Yes, but I probably shouldn't have said all the time. He does get a call every single night from his brother in Baltimore, and that's just to mention one."

Shayne stopped smiling abruptly. "Baltimore? Are you sure?"

"Oh, yes. It comes in around six-thirty. Ordinarily I wouldn't know if a call was local or long distance, but one night there was a mix-up in the circuits, and I heard the Baltimore operator trying to straighten it out."

Another light flashed on her board. As she was attending to it, Rose came up behind Shayne.

"There you are," she said.

Shayne lighted his cigarette. "You have an uncle in Baltimore, I hear."

"Of course I don't. I have one uncle here in town and one on the West Coast."

Shayne went on smoking until the operator was free. He

asked her, "Are you sure this Baltimore call was one of the regular six-thirty calls from his brother?"

She smiled. "Oh, we're on quite friendly terms by now. This was only a few days after Mr. Chadwick came here from the hospital. When I found out it was an out-of-town call, I asked him why he didn't make it person-to-person, and then if his brother couldn't answer the phone, the call wouldn't be completed and it wouldn't cost him anything. But he said he'd rather talk to somebody and find out if there'd been any change, one way or the other."

"How did he identify himself?" Shayne said.

"The first couple of times, just that he was John Chadwick, Mr. Chadwick's brother. After that I recognized his voice."

"What kind of voice is it?"

"I wouldn't know how to describe it, Mr. Shayne. Sort of deep, no particular accent."

Shayne looked at Rose. "Do you have an Uncle John?"

"He's the one in California. He's seventy-nine, and he hasn't done any traveling in years. He's called me at home a few times, and he knows I'll phone him if there's any news. He wouldn't call here. It must be somebody using his name."

Shayne looked at his watch, a plan taking shape in his head. "Who's the doctor in charge, Rose? This may be just the break we've been waiting for."

13

SIX-THIRTY CAME and went. Each time the switchboard buzzed, the operator glanced nervously at Shayne before she threw the switch and took the call. Each time, after listening to the first few words, she shook her head. Rose, at the office desk across the room, was smoking one cigarette after another.

At 6:45 there was another buzz. "Sunset Nursing Home, good evening," she said, and an instant later she looked at Shayne and nodded excitedly. Shayne picked up the office phone, which was already plugged in. He heard a man's voice: "John Chadwick again, and good evening to you. A little late tonight, but it couldn't be helped. Any news?"

The girl was so excited that she stammered "Y-yes, yes, there is, Mr. Chadwick, there certainly is. We're all so glad, I can't begin to tell you."

"Good news?" the voice said tensely. "That's wonderful! The paralysis?"

"Even better than that. Naturally we want him to be perfectly well again, and he's still having some trouble with his left side. But the wonderful thing is that he's going to be able to talk!"

"I should say it is wonderful," the voice said heartily. "Almost too good to be true."

"That's what we all think here. Dr. Shoifett is terribly gratified, because he's been using an experimental treatment, which only works about ten percent of the time. I was hoping you'd call earlier so you could talk to the doctor, but he just left this minute. Mr. Chadwick said his first words about two hours ago. It was pretty fuzzy, but according to Dr. Shoifett that's not the point. If the throat muscles function at all, eventual recovery is almost certain."

She looked at Shayne, who gave her an encouraging nod. Rose was leaning forward, fingers laced.

The voice said, "That's great. I'm having trouble taking it in. His mind was clear? He recognized people?"

"I'd better not try to be definite on that," she said. "I got the impression from the nurses that—but I'd better let you talk to Dr. Shoifett in the morning. The patient's been given a strong sedative and he's sleeping soundly. I probably shouldn't have said as much as I have, but it's so nice to be able to give somebody some encouraging news, for a change. Maybe the next time you call you can talk to him yourself."

"I'm certainly looking forward to that. Was my niece with him when he—"

The girl looked at Shayne, who shook his head.

"No, she wasn't, Mr. Chadwick. She came over right away, but he was asleep by the time she got here."

The man on the phone repeated that his brother's recovery of speech seemed almost a miracle, and thanked the girl several times before he hung up. She closed the switch and blew out her breath in a long sigh.

"Did I say anything wrong?"

"You were perfect," Shayne said.

Rose had put her clasped hands to her forehead. Her eyes were closed. Shayne touched her shoulder.

"Don't think about it, Rose. It may still actually happen."

She shook her head helplessly. "It's not that. I know he's no more or less sick than he was before. It's just that—using him like this—"

"I wouldn't do it if I could think of any better way," Shayne said. "He'd agree if we could explain it to him. More than one life is at stake. He won't be in any danger. He'll be in another part of town."

She looked up. "There's danger to you."

"That's what I'm paid for. Now let's work this out with Wing."

She touched his sleeve. "Can't I sleep in one of the third-floor rooms? With you here I'll be as safe as I would be by myself in some hotel. I'd go out of my mind anywhere else."

"We can decide that after Joe Wing gets here."

He asked the switchboard girl for an outside line. He was passed along from one number to another until he reached Joe Wing at a restaurant near the jail.

"Shayne," the redhead said. "We've had some developments, and if you want to take part you'd better rearrange your schedule and come in to the Sunset Nursing Home off West Avenue."

"I know the place," Wing said. "Be more specific, can't you, Mike? I just sat down to dinner. I was going back to the jail to spell the sheriff. He's asked the same questions so many times he's getting punchdrunk."

"Why don't you do that, Joe?" Shayne said with a grin. "I'll take care of it, and if I catch the guy I'll call you right away."

"All right, all right," Wing said with resignation. "Tell them to make some coffee. I'll be right there."

"We'll need another man," Shayne said. "And you might stop at a drugstore and pick up some benzedrine."

"Oh, it's going to be one of those nights, is it?" Wing said. "It's going to take more than benzedrine to keep *me* awake. I'm so tired I couldn't even tell you my own name."

After Shayne hung up he said, "Nothing can happen till after dark. We have time to eat. And we're going to need lots and lots of coffee."

"Wait in the dining room," the switchboard girl said. "I'll see that they take care of you."

Wing arrived as Shayne was pouring a second cup of coffee.

"Just black for me, please," Wing said. "Hello, Mrs. Heminway. Tell me what's going on, Mike, and it better be interesting."

"Anytime I start boring you, let me know," Shayne told him. "Mrs. Heminway's Uncle John has been calling up every night around six-thirty to find out if Chadwick has been doing any talking, only he's not really Uncle John. And one of his calls was long distance from Baltimore."

"Well, well," Wing said, ignoring his coffee. "You're not boring me so far."

"When he called tonight, I had the girl tell him his prayers had been answered. Chadwick had said a couple of words. Just a couple, and then the doctor gave him a sedative. In the morning we're all pretty sure he'll be his old self again."

"That's taking quite a lot on yourself, Mike," Wing grumbled. "I wish you'd cleared it with me first."

"I found out about it at six-twenty-five. I didn't have time. Of course if you don't approve of the idea we can always put a sign on his door that it was just a piece of good clean fun."

"Now Mike. I just wish I'd been told about it. What about the officials here?"

"We have to persuade them. Rather, you have to persuade them. There has to be a certain amount of shifting around of patients, and we'll need your authority for that. Chadwick ought to be moved to another hospital for the night, and we'll need his room and the room on each side."

"What makes you think the guy knows Chadwick's room number?"

"He's gone to a lot of trouble. He wouldn't overlook a thing like that."

Wing left his coffee half-finished and went to find the director. When he came back he was more enthusiastic.

"How's the coffee, still hot? I hate to admit it, Mike, but the reason I didn't jump at this right away was because it wasn't my idea. I don't see any reason why it shouldn't work. That voice on the phone almost has to belong to the same guy who had Fred Milburn stabbed and sent the boys to shoot Mrs. Heminway. Chadwick must know something he was about to spill to Painter. It all comes back to Painter." He looked soberly at the fresh coffee he had just poured. "And

I've just about come to the conclusion that we aren't going to find Painter in one piece."

"No!" Rose cried.

Wing went on, still looking down into his coffee. "If only the jerk had told somebody what he was doing! It's bad when a cop as important as Painter gets killed. It's like losing a battle. The city won't clamp down for months."

"He also happens to be a person," Rose said quietly.

"Well, yes. Technically I suppose you're right, but that's never the first thing that comes to mind when you think about Peter Painter."

"Did you fix things with the doctor?" Shayne said.

"Yeah. He's sending Chadwick to Jackson Memorial. I'm moving into Chadwick's room. You can use the room on one side, Mike. I brought Norton with me, and he can use the other."

"This was my idea," Shayne said. "I'll be in Chadwick's room."

"Out of the question, Mike."

Shayne smiled. "You're in charge. There was something I wanted to tell you—what was it? Oh, yes. Four boys from the St. Albans were seen chasing Petey up Collins last night around nine in a Drive-Urself Chevy. But you'll be busy here. I'll work on that angle."

Wing ran his fingers distractedly through his hair. "I begin to get an idea why Painter felt the way he did about you, Mike. I wish I could end up ahead of you once. Just once, that's all I ask. Okay, you win. Let's have it."

An ambulance arrived for Rose's father. She had persuaded Lieutenant Wing to let her stay, and she had been assigned to an unoccupied room on the top floor, under the eaves. Shayne drove to the nearest bar for a bottle of cognac, and then put his Buick in the garage where it wouldn't be seen; beside Wing's police car. Wing, meanwhile, had been giving orders by phone. There would be nearly as many police covering the Truckers' convention as there were formal delegates. Names and descriptions of the four men Kincaid had seen had been circulated—one name and one nickname, and not much in the way of descriptions—and Shayne didn't think there was much hope that they would turn up any sooner than Painter himself.

Gradually the Sunset Nursing Home settled down for the night. The last visitor left. The doctor made his evening rounds, and lights began to blink out.

Rose told Shayne goodnight at the bottom of the stairs to the third floor.

"I know it's a lot to ask you, but *please* be careful, Mike. I know it's your business, I know you wouldn't be in it if you didn't enjoy it, but I couldn't forgive myself if anything happened to you."

"Get some sleep, Rose."

"Sleep!"

She started up the stairs, then turned suddenly and came in against him hard. Her arms went around him.

"Mike," she whispered. "I don't want to ask you anything, but—the reason I wanted to stay here was so if you—wanted to—I get so lonely, so scared, in bed by myself. Oh, darling."

She raised her mouth to his and pressed her body against him.

"Mike, can't you, please? For a little while. He wouldn't come yet, not till much later."

"No, Rose," Shayne said. "Everything has to be set. There can't be any moving around."

She looked at him seriously and whispered, "Then tomorrow?" Coloring slightly in the dim light, she turned and ran upstairs.

Shayne went thoughtfully down the long corridor, making a mental note of something else he didn't expect to tell Lucy Hamilton. As he came abreast of the room next to Chadwick's, the door opened and Wing looked out. He was in his shirt sleeves, his shoulder holster showing.

"You took your time, Mike," he said. "I ate enough Bennies to stay awake for three weeks, and let's just hope they work. I'm going to sit in a straight chair next to the door, so I can't fall asleep without falling down. That's a noisy latch on your door. Let's wait till the guy opens the door before we grab him."

"Fine, Joe. I'm going to rig up something that will make a racket when the door opens. And don't use that gun except to make him stand still. We want to talk to this man."

"I'm no rookie, for God's sake."

In the room on the other side, Norton was prowling around in his stocking feet. Shayne looked in on him, then went into the room he was going to use. He plumped up the covers of the narrow hospital bed to make it seem that someone was sleeping there, and balanced a pair of scissors on the doorknob in such a way that it would be knocked off when the knob was turned. The kitchen had sent up a large pot of coffee and an electric burner. Shayne poured a cup of coffee, added cognac and sipped it slowly. Then he turned out the lamp.

The room was on the second floor, facing south. Not much light came through the single window except when a car, coming along West Avenue, made the turn onto Biscayne Street. There would be a moon, but it was not yet up. Shayne waited until his eyes adjusted to the darkness. Then he began moving about the room, getting used to the position of the furniture. There wasn't much furniture to worry about—a bureau, a standing lamp and two chairs.

He moved one of the chairs to the wall near the door and sat down. The air-conditioning unit was humming quietly. He decided not to risk a cigarette. The patient who usually occupied this room, being paralyzed, naturally didn't smoke. There was a smell of coffee, but it couldn't be helped; Shayne couldn't get through a second sleepless night without the help of coffee.

The moon rose. It was three-quarters full. Shayne lowered the Venetian blind and tilted the slats, and poured another cup of coffee. He managed to kill fifteen minutes with that one cup. The night was very quiet, and he could hear Norton moving restlessly in the next room. After putting the cup on the bureau beside the pot he took several turns back and forth from the window to the door. He was fully awake, but the instant he sat down again he went into a light doze. The slightest sound at the door would have awakened him, but when there was a faint metallic clink at the window an hour or so later, it didn't penetrate.

The sound was repeated. Shayne heard it this time, but still half asleep, he didn't react. He even knew what had made the sound—a chisel being forced between the air-conditioner and the sash. Then the sash came up, and at that moment several things happened at once.

The moon had slipped behind clouds, but a car threw its headlights against the window, and through the tilted slats of the blind Shayne saw an all-black figure, wearing what seemed to be a tight black jersey. Something dropped into the room. Even before the headlights flashed past, the figure was gone.

Shayne sprang to his feet and called, "*Joe! Outside!*"

He ran to the window and wrenched at the partly-raised sash. But it was jammed. He knew he was overlooking something important, and perhaps a second and a half passed before he realized what it was. Without an instant's further thought he drew back a step and threw himself at the window.

He had raised his arm as he plunged forward, twisting to protect his eyes and face. His elbow struck the blind with the full force of his powerful body behind it. The blind came loose with a crash, glass and wood splintered. Shayne fell through onto the veranda roof, and at that instant there was a terrific explosion inside the room.

He had brought part of the blind with him. The momentum of his diving fall carried him to the edge of the roof, where he grabbed at the gutter to check himself. He was in precarious balance for a second, but the broken-off section of the blind whipped past him and carried him on over. Snared in the ropes, he landed badly, on his side with one arm beneath him. Each noise had overlapped with the next, and the whole thing had almost seemed to happen at once, as though the shattering of the glass, the clatter of the blind as it came down, his awkward fall, had all been part of the same explosion. For a moment he couldn't move. He lay amid the wreckage, surrounded by ropes and torn slats and pieces of wood, looking up at the sky and swearing under his breath. Then he came to his feet. "Joe!" he yelled.

He heard the pounding of footsteps inside the building. He crouched, listening. He couldn't be sure how much time had passed since the bomb had been thrown into the room. Perhaps he had blacked out for a moment; perhaps not. He started for the corner of the house, and one of the Venetian blind ropes tightened around his ankle and threw him.

He freed himself, swearing more savagely. The porch-light flashed on. Joe Wing ran out, a gun in his hand.

"Hold it!" Shayne yelled as the gun came up.

"Mike! What are you doing out *here?*"

"What do you think, catching fireflies? Do you hear anything?"

Wing listened. But by now there was too much noise from the house to hear anything. Norton charged out through the door. Apparently he had reached Shayne's room in time to run into the blast; his shirt was ripped, his face blackened. He, too, was waving a gun, to Shayne's disgust.

Lights were coming on all over the building. Suddenly a woman's voice screamed.

"He's got some kind of a black sweater on," Shayne said. "Black pants. Maybe we can still—"

He set off up the driveway at a hard run. The iron gates were open; probably they were never closed. Shayne ran through and looked both ways. Several cars were parked on the drive nearby. When Norton joined him, Shayne said brusquely, "Check those parked cars. Then watch the gate."

He turned back and met Wing as the lieutenant ran up the driveway toward him. "He can't be far away," Shayne said. "I haven't heard a car."

"We'll have a couple of patrols here in a minute," Wing said. "What kind of a sweater is he wearing?"

"Black jersey, skin-tight."

"You're bleeding like a pig, Mike."

"Too bad," Shayne said. "Let's find this son of a bitch and then I'll get a transfusion."

They separated. Shayne had no trouble so long as he was out on the lawn, but he had to move cautiously when he went among the shrubs and bushes at the edge of the nursing home property. Reaching the high iron fence, protected at its base by a thick barberry hedge, he turned back toward the water. Off to his left, Wing's flashlight moved back in the direction of the house. Many of the windows were lighted, and Shayne saw the gaping hole he had left as he crashed through the window ahead of the explosion.

A little crowd of patients and attendants had gathered on the porch under the overhead light. Sirens were wailing. Soon the bushes became too dense to move through without a light, and Shayne went back to the lawn. As he came into the light from the porch, Rose broke from the others and ran toward him.

"Mike! You—"

She stopped, aghast at what she saw. Shayne brushed the blood out of his eyes.

Suddenly, beneath the excited rattle of conversation from the porch, he noticed another sound—the quiet beating of an inboard motor, and then he knew the explanation of the tight black jersey.

"A skin-diver!" he shouted to Wing, who was coming out of the shrubbery on the other side of the lawn. "He swam out to a boat. Call the Coast Guard."

14

THE COAST GUARD station at the end of the MacArthur Causeway turned out three patrol boats, and turned them out in a hurry. They crisscrossed the bay from the mainland to the southern tip of the Beach, but Shayne, watching their searchlights from the side porch of the nursing home, knew that they were too late. It was impressive, the kind of massive effort that couldn't be mounted by a single private detective, but if the bomber had slipped through before the boats were in position, as Shayne was sure he had, it was wasted effort.

Dr. Shoiffet had patched Shayne up, removing several fragments of broken glass and taking several stitches in the worst gash, over one eye. He had wrenched his left shoulder, and it was beginning to stiffen. Lieutenant Wing and an explosives expert were working in the bombed-out room. Apparently the bomber had known the exact location of Chadwick's bed. Looking at the twisted wreckage, Wing congratulated Shayne dryly on not having been in it. Morton, hearing Shayne's call, had rushed out, and the bomb had gone off when he was wrenching at the doorknob. The door was blown off its hinges and came back in his face, shielding him from the full force of the blast.

Rose and most of the patients had gone back to bed and things were beginning to quiet down. The night had four hours to run and Michael Shayne was feeling the pressure. He was pacing restlessly up and down the porch when a car drove up to the front steps and Tim Rourke piled out.

His face was puffy with lack of sleep, and he hadn't taken the time or trouble to button all the buttons of his shirt. His skinny chest could be seen through the gaps. He ran his fingers through his hair, which was all the maintenance he usually gave it.

"Hey, Mike," he said. "You look grisly. Fighting again?"

"You should see the other guy," Shayne said sourly. "Not a mark on him."

"You had an explosion out here, they tell me."

"Second floor," the redhead said briefly. "You can't miss it."

"Don't go anywhere, Mike. Any chance of a drink in this place?"

"I had a bottle of cognac upstairs," Shayne said. "But I don't think there's much left of either the cognac or the bottle."

"There must be a doctor around. This is a nursing home, isn't it? I'll hit him for some prescription stuff."

Shayne went on pacing while Rourke visited the scene of the explosion and phoned his paper. He came out fifteen minutes later, an unlighted cigarette dangling from his lips.

"This quack they have here doesn't think he'd advise a drink. Let's go to my place, Mike. I keep a couple of pints in the bottom of the laundry hamper, for emergencies."

"Later," Shayne said.

"Later! Two nights in a row is a little too much. I'm an old man. I get tired."

"Sit down," Shayne said.

Something in his friend's tone seemed to surprise Rourke; he sat down obediently in one of the wicker rocking chairs. Shayne planted himself on the broad porch railing.

"I've picked up a few things," Shayne said, "but there's still a long way to go. You said something this morning—no, hell, *yesterday* morning—that might ring a loud bell if I could only remember what it was."

Rourke scowled. "That's about the vaguest remark I ever heard from you."

"I know it's vague!" Shayne said angrily. "But let's see if

we can find it. I think it was when we were talking about the Truckers' election. Anything new on that?"

"They've been wheeling and dealing all day," Rourke said, lighting his cigarette. "They pulled me off the story to cover a knifing in the county jail. And I understand you were on the premises at the time, far too busy to put in a phone call to your old pal Tim Rourke. I'm not complaining. I'm not asking questions. I'm just touching lightly on one of those areas where the press would like a little explanation."

"Keep your mind on the union election. Does Plato still look good for the Welfare Fund?"

"The last I heard. There's a bunch of sub-bosses who'd like to dump him because he's been getting such lousy publicity, but they don't have a chance unless they can get Quinn to go along. My informants tell me he's been getting some handsome offers, but he's still in Plato's corner."

"Baltimore. That's come up a couple of times now. Are the Baltimore delegates part of any faction?"

"I'd have to ask. It's part of the Eastern district, and that's Quinn's. But Plato's got strength all over the country. He's in Washington a lot of the time, which isn't far from Baltimore."

"This goon named Al Cole, the boy with the Lüger. Does he fit anywhere?"

"That was attempted murder, Mike. I've got a couple of cooperative sources in the union, but they don't talk to reporters about things like that."

"The guy who tossed the bomb upstairs was wearing a skin-diver's outfit. You've probably read the biographies of all the top men. Do you remember anybody with that kind of hobby?"

"Not offhand. When these guys relax they usually do it in a nightclub, with a couple of babes to improve the scenery. Of course they all have boats. That's the big status symbol these days. The bigger the boat, the bigger the status. But when they put to sea they take along a case of liquor and the usual couple of babes, so it's not much different from going to a nightclub."

Shayne had been watching the searchlights move across water. Now he swung around on Rourke. "That's it! When you were telling me about Plato you said he had a boat."

"It's no secret. I forget how many she sleeps, enough to keep one man busy, anyway. I can remember the name if I think hard enough. *The Panther!* He sailed down on her. The Washington reporters all wanted to talk to him about the convention, but Plato, who in some ways is a very smart apple, couldn't be reached. He was at sea."

Shayne was snapping his fingers silently. Rouke said, watching him, "An idea?"

"You're goddam right! That's where he took Painter!"

Rourke screwed up his eyes. "So that's who's got Painter. Thanks for telling me."

"I don't know for sure," Shayne said impatiently. "But Petey was last seen going up Collins last night with four of Plato's huskies behind him in a rented Chevy." He stood for a moment looking down at the reporter. "Let's go find the boat."

Rourke didn't answer for a moment. "Taking a few cops with us, of course."

"Not taking any cops. You know what the rum-runners used to do when they saw a revenue cutter. They dumped their cargo. I wouldn't want that to happen to Petey, and it's what will happen if a few carloads of cops show up at dockside with their sirens going. First we find him. Then we look the situation over. Then we'll talk about how much help we'll need, if any."

"If any," Rourke said. "That's what I'm afraid of. And how do we find this needle in the haystack? There are more marinas in town these days than motels. And it is now, unless my watch has stopped because of all the excitement—" he consulted the time—"three o'clock in the morning."

"He'd use a marina on the Beach or one of the islands, to be handy to the St. Albans. I doubt if they'd let him in a yacht club, so we can skip those. If he owns a luxury boat, he'd tie up at a luxury dock. That cuts it down. If the name is the Panther she's probably painted black."

"That's sound reasoning, old man, except that we ran a picture when he came in, and she's painted white. A couple of decks amidships, I don't know what they're called, plenty of cabin-space and a big mast. And one of those forward platforms over the bow for catching tuna. She's not as big as the Queens, but in the ordinary marina I admit she'd tend to stick out."

"Now you're being helpful, Tim. You start at the south end of the Beach, I'll start at the north, and we'll meet in the middle."

"Tell you what, Mike. This is more your idea than it is mine. I don't want anything too bad to happen to Painter, but I don't want anything to happen to me, either. I'll be home. If you find the boat and decide you need help, call me."

"Sure," Shayne said carelessly. "If you want to know how it turns out, buy a *Herald* in the morning."

"You're mixed up, Mike. The *News* is my paper."

"I'm not mixed up."

"Mike! How can you do a thing like this to me?" He struggled up out of the rocking chair. "You mentioned four goons. You and me make two. We're outnumbered. Couldn't we take a *couple* of cops? If they promise to walk tiptoe?"

"No," Shayne said curtly.

"Do I say goodnight to Wing?"

"He's busy. Let's not disturb him."

They started down the steps. Rourke shook his head. "Mike, did you really dive headfirst out of a second-floor window?"

"Yeah, I really did."

"I wish I'd been here to see it. You must have made quite a splash."

Shayne backed his Buick out of the garage. Rourke let him pass, and followed. Speeding down Biscayne Street with Rourke's headlights gleaming in his rear-view mirror, the big redhead went back over everything he knew about the case, skirting the large gaps in his knowledge and those places where experience told him that he had been listening to lies. Harry Plato, he knew, would kidnap a policeman only if it was absolutely vital to him, but the conviction was growing in Shayne that his sudden hunch had been right, that Plato, a stranger in town, surrounded by enemies, could find no better place to hide his prisoner than aboard a boat. And at that point Shayne put the unanswered questions aside for consideration later, and with characteristic concentration, planned the search.

At the corner of Collins Avenue, Tim Rourke blinked his lights and turned to the right. Shayne continued all the way north on Collins, making good time in the light traffic. Reaching Haulover Beach Park, he parked and walked over to the bayfront, where he began the slow, laborious process of checking marinas. He would walk casually past on the promenade, keeping to an easy saunter, as though he was a guest at one of the big hotels further south, unable to sleep and out for a stroll in the moonlight. One eye was cocked for a tall white boat with a mast and a tuna-rig. Part of the time the moon was behind clouds, but when it was out the visibility was good. He saw white boats of the shape Rourke had described, he saw radio masts, he saw several of the awkward tuna platforms, looking like afterthoughts, but he didn't see them all together.

He went back to the Buick and moved it down to Bal Harbour. Here there were fewer possibilities and he made better time. Passing the 79th Street Causeway, he parked again and walked the short block to the water, where he knew he would find one of the largest and best-equipped marinas in the North Bay. There was a large clubhouse in the middle of a plaza, with four long docks sticking out in the water like the outstretched fingers of a hand.

He went to the water's edge and his eye ran along the long rows of berths, all but a few of them filled. The boats were every size and shape and color. His eye was caught by a white boat near the end of the northernmost dock. The silhouette was right, but there was no tuna platform. He looked past, but kept coming back. Those platforms could be unbolted and stowed, and perhaps, Shayne thought, it had been taken off after Plato's arrival in Miami. Certainly this pretentious monster was just the kind Harry Plato would choose when he was shopping for boats.

Shayne moved on to the north, avoiding the clubhouse. Again he looked out over the water. Clouds were scudding across the moon. He was too far away from the white boat to make out her name, but he saw the capital P, counted letters and saw the rise of the "t" and "h" in the middle. *Panther*!

He threw away his cigarette and crossed the street at an angle, heading for the place where he had left his Buick. He passed between two parked cars. As he came out on the sidewalk, two men stepped in against him from either side, and one of them hit his injured side with the muzzle of a gun. The redhead straightened his arms in an instinctive reflex, getting both hands out in the moonlight where they could be seen.

One of the men said, "Do something stupid and we'll use you for target practice. I'm going to get your billfold. Keep your hands where they are."

Shayne turned his head carefully to look at the man who had spoken. He was about Shayne's size, six feet two and built as solidly as a professional football tackle. There was a ridge of scar tissue over his eyes. The other was the bald man Shayne had seen in Plato's sitting room. He kept jabbing Shayne's side with the gun. The door of a parked car opened and somebody else came out. The redhead didn't look that way, but saved him for later.

"Stop pushing me with that thing," Shayne said evenly, "or you'll have to shoot me with it."

"I won't mind," the man told him.

The big man patted Shayne lightly on the hips and under the arms, slid one hand inside Shayne's coat and took out his wallet. The man holding the gun stepped backward while the other held the wallet to the moonlight.

"I told you it was Mike Shayne," he said.

"You boys owe me ten bucks apiece," a voice said behind Shayne. He looked around and saw a small, neatly dressed man with a badly eroded face, who was smiling cheerfully. "When I heard you were in on this I knew you'd turn up, Shayne. Just a matter of time."

"Yeah, but how in God's name did he—" the man with the gun said.

"Maybe I tipped him off so I could collect the twenty bucks," the small man said. "What difference does it make? Do you like boats, Shayne? We're having a little party aboard. I know you'll enjoy it."

"I'm in no mood for a party," Shayne said.

The big man with the gun grinned. "The party's in the mood for you."

"Turn around, Shayne," the small man said. "There's three of us, and you're the only one here without a gun. Draw your own conclusions. Keep holding your hands just that way."

Shayne said, puzzled, "I don't get it. How much money is in this Welfare Fund Harry's trying to get hold of?"

"Plenty. Stick it in his ribs again, Whizzer. Give him a jab with it now and then. One thing I've heard about him, he's not too impressed with being on the short end of the odds."

Whizzer started forward, and Shayne said quickly, "Somebody's been telling lies about me. I'm realistic. Put the gun away."

He stepped off the curb, between the cars. This was the only chance he'd get to deal with them one by one. He stumbled and went headlong, landing on his hands. Twisting, he lashed out with one foot and caught the man named Whizzer in the soft flesh above the knee. In the same motion he doubled forward, coming underneath the gun as it swung down at him. His big hand glanced from the barrel and knocked it skyward, and his other hand fastened on Whizzer's wrist.

Shayne's powerful body uncoiled in one continuous, fluid movement, driving upward beneath the gun, and slammed a hard right against the side of Whizzer's jaw. The blow had started from the pavement, picking up speed as it went. Whizzer went sideward against the front grill of the nearest car, making a sound like air escaping from a balloon. Shayne still had him by the wrist. He swung him like a door, aiming at the big man, who was trying to get in position to make his size and weight count.

"Grab him, Jack!" the small man cried.

Whizzer's feet left the ground. He crashed into Jack, the big man, who tripped against the curb and went down. Shayne whirled. The small man had danced away. He had a gun out and was waving it back and forth.

"Stand still, you dumb Mick," he said softly.

Shayne snarled. The big man had thrown Whizzer off and was coming up at him. Shayne sidestepped, to get the man's bulk between him and the gun. He evaded a high punch to the head, blocked another to the body, and catching the other around the waist, wrestled him backward, trying to force him against the gun.

"Don't try to out-slug him, Jack!" the smaller man shouted. "Just hang onto him."

The big man, cursing steadily, wrapped one of his long arms around Shayne and began working on his mid-section with his right. The small man darted past and cracked Shayne's head sharply with the flat of the pistol. The big man drove two more hard rights against Shayne's body. The redhead's strength was beginning to go. Then the man with the gun reversed it and brought the butt-plate down on Shayne's skull.

He didn't go all the way out, but he came close. He sank to his knees. The big man continued to work on his body with his right. Shayne heard the small man's voice: "That's all, Jack. That's all. We don't want to have to carry him."

Shayne's brain turned over weakly. "What was the last name? Klipstone?"

It came out in a kind of mumble, but they heard him.

"What's that?" the small man said sharply.

Klipstone said, "The bastard's too educated. I want to work him over some more when we get him aboard. I won't make any noise."

"Let's not start shifting strategy at this date, for God's sake," his companion said. "Get him up."

"How about Whizzer?"

"He can lie there till he can move by himself. He deserves some hard pavement for hanging his jaw out like that. Jesus! I thought for a minute Shayne was going to get away from us, and that would really be something, you know?"

Shayne could hear what they were saying, but he didn't have much command over his arms and legs. Klipstone lifted him to the fender of the nearest car.

"Hold him there," the small man said. He came close to Shayne. "You made your point. You're a big tough man and how you trailed us here without dogs I'd like somebody to tell me sometime. You're probably a pretty good detective. Congratulations. Are you hearing me?"

"I hear you," Shayne mumbed through numb lips.

"Act intelligent and maybe you'll live through this. Act dumb and I can tell you for sure—you get dropped in the bay. It's that simple. We've got something big going here, and there's too much involved to kid around. Now on your feet."

Shayne swayed away from the fender. With Klipstone no longer holding him, he pitched forward, turning as he fell so he would land on his uninjured shoulder. Oddly, the shock cleared his mind and he was able to look at the question soberly; should he try to walk by himself, or make them carry him?

The small man solved it for him. Stooping down, he slapped Shayne with his gun, just hard enough to sting him. Shayne lurched to his feet. Klipstone let him lean on him as they crossed the street to the marina entrance. Shayne swung his head toward the office as they passed. The watchman's head and shoulders lay on his desk, an uncorked bottle of Scotch beside him. They headed down the long dock between the boats. The small man took Shayne's arm to hurry him along.

The dizziness was passing off, but he continued to lean on Klipstone, for any advantage it might bring him later. As they approached the large white boat, Shayne saw the lettering on the broad stern change from a blur to "Panther, New Orleans."

Another man, wearing nothing but a pair of tattered shorts, heavily-muscled and tattooed, came out of the shadows of the deck-house. He caught Shayne as he was thrust aboard.

"Take a good look, Mac," the small man said, jumping down on the deck. "This is the well-known Michael Shayne. He tried to take all three of us, and he damn near did it, too. Put him below."

"Okay, Mr. Gray. In the same cabin?"

"Why not? Shayne seems to know all our little secrets. How is he?"

"I'd say he's starting to slobber."

"Well, he's got a bigger capacity than I gave him credit for. Glad to have you aboard, Shayne."

Shayne gave him a piece of rude advice, and he raised his eyebrows, pretending to be shocked. "Such language."

The tattooed man spun Shayne around and thrust him into a companionway. The stairs were very steep, and Shayne descended them carefully. He had taken enough falls for one night. At the bottom, a tattooed arm reached past his shoulder and unlocked a door. Shayne was pushed into a small cabin. A light was on, but the porthole on this side faced toward the bay, which was why he hadn't seen it from the shore. He heard the door being locked behind him.

The cabin's furniture consisted of a double bunk, a table and a chair. Someone lay in the lower bunk, and Shayne was not really surprised to see that it was Peter Painter. His usual dapper figure was a shambles. He still wore a necktie, cinched up tightly, but his shirt was open all the way down to the belt-buckle. A highball glass was balanced on his chest. He wore no shoes and only one sock, the garter flapping. His head turned and he looked at Shayne. "Hi, Mike," he said amiably.

Then he came up off the bunk as though he had received

an electric shock at the base of the spine. The highball spilled and he cracked his forehead on the underside of the upper bunk. He clapped his hand to the injured spot and swung his feet out.

"Shayne! I've been looking all over. Where have you been, you bastard? You're under arrest!"

15

PAINTER POINTED AN accusing finger at Shayne and waved wildly with the other arm, as though calling up reserves. "I arrest you for breaking and entering and attempted manslaughter, and that's only the start, by God! I've been waiting for this for years. Now I've got you where I want you, and I'm going to make you squeal!"

Shayne laughed. "Take it easy, Petey." He picked up an article of women's underclothing from a chair and dangled it in the air for a moment before letting it drop. "I see they're taking good care of you. And to think we've been worrying."

Painter's mood changed abruptly. "I know all about it. You and your hoodlum friends think you're going to get me drunk, do you? I'm too smart for you."

Shayne put one hip on the table and repeated skeptically, "You're too smart for us."

"Somebody comes in every half hour and pours me some more gin." He chortled. "Only what they don't know is that I don't really drink it, I let it trickle down my chin. Clever?"

"You're just pretending," Shayne said.

"Oh, I take a sip now and then to make it look good, but I'm one jump ahead all the time. I know what you're planning for the morning. You're going to dump me in a motel, stinking of gin, with a lot of empties and some ladies' underwear, you dirty-minded so-and-sos. Goodbye career. Out on a bat when I should be attending to business. It takes a real psycho to think of something like that, and I know whose idea it was, too. Yours—you sadist! But you didn't expect me to outguess you, did you? You always underestimate my intelligence. I saw through the whole thing when I found those—those—"

"Pants," Shayne said.

"Pants. Yes. But you never should have tangled with me, Shayne. I'm sold cone stober, that's what give me my advantage."

He let go of the railing to make a more emphatic gesture, and fell to the floor. Shayne picked him up.

Painter murmured, "Slippery wax." He peered at Shayne. "Okay, now make a new plan, damn you. I'll outfox you again. You had sense enough not to show your face all day, and it's lucky for you, boy. Right now I happen to be a little tired, but wait till I get my strength back."

"You're not making much sense, Petey," Shayne told him. "Is there any more gin?"

"May be a bottle round somewhere, but I'm not giving *you* any of it. I always knew you were low. But these aren't just juvenile delinquents or something. They're killers and big thieves, and I never figured you to throw in with an outfit like this for a few lousy bucks. I guess I'm an idealist, but I figured you for a few scruples. Not many, just a few. How's Heinemann?"

"He was okay the last time I saw him," Shayne said.

"And Gray? I suppose he's okay, too?"

Shayne shrugged. "If you mean the little guy with the pockmarks, there were two others in the way and I didn't get around to him."

"Oh, no. You just opened his scalp to the bone, that's all. I hope the ambulance got there in time—or do I? If he kicked off, I get you for murder in the second, and that's more satisfying than manslaughter."

Shayne saw a square bottle sticking out from beneath the bunk, and he captured it. There were still two fingers of gin in the bottom. He swirled it around once and drank it, while Painter, from the bunk, watched indignantly.

"Did I say you were low?" Painter cried. "I suppose it didn't occur to you to offer me some?"

"You've had enough," Shayne said, tossing the empty bottle into the top bunk.

"You think so, do you? I'm not even getting started. You think you can hold your liquor better than ordinary people, don't you? There's a few drops in a bottle, and you hog it all. I don't care how much they're paying you! You made a bad mistake this time. You can't break into apartments and rob people's files and slug Senate investigators and sucker a police officer in the performance of his duty and get away with it, and you'll find that out in a hurry!"

"Cut the clowning, Petey. I don't need you to tell me that people have been killed by this bunch. If we're going to get out of this mess, you've got to start talking sense."

Painter ran out of steam all at once. He said helplessly, "I thought this was one time I was ahead of you. *How did you know?*"

"Know what?" Shayne said.

"That I had the real story on the Beach Trust robbery. What was it, instinct?"

"We'll get to that in a minute. Who's this Senate investigator you think I slugged?"

"I only think you slugged him? I see. It wasn't anything but a hallucination. You didn't break into my apartment. You didn't tear the place to pieces. Certainly not. You didn't take me on a wild-goose chase up Collins, and lead me into a dead-end so your pals could grab me. Oh, no. Four of them—they came at me from all sides at once—I didn't have a chance to defend myself—four to one, real sporting of you, Shayne. But that wasn't you. You're too law-abiding."

Shayne was trying hard to make sense of this. "Will you go through that again, Petey? Slowly?"

"I'm surprised you deny it. It worked, and that's the main thing, isn't it? I thought you'd be bragging about it. I have eyes, after all. It was your license number."

Shayne said sharply, "You were chasing a car with my tag?"

"*A* car, hell. *Your* car. I recognized it even without the number."

Shayne's mouth was grim. "You were suckered, all right. I left my car outside a Beach saloon. Somebody must have borrowed it."

Painter sneered weakly. "How dumb do you think I am?"

"Pretty goddam dumb," Shayne said, "if you think I'm fronting for killers. Why did I do all this?"

"For money! You'd sell your best friend, if the price tag was right, and I'm not your best friend, as everybody knows."

"That's true," Shayne said. "The more I see of you, the less I like you. And while we're on the subject of no-brains, if you found some evidence to clear Sam Harris, why in God's name have you been sitting on it?"

"I had my reasons," Painter said smugly.

"They'd better be good. Because as a direct result of your damn foolishness, a man named Fred Milburn was killed, a hood from Baltimore tried to take a shot at Rose Heminway and came pretty close to doing it, somebody else blew up Benjamin Chadwick's room at his nursing home. But you're not dumb. No, you're brilliant. They'll write about you in *Argosy*."

Painter looked at him, blinking. "Somebody shot at Rose? But why would anybody—?"

"That's one of the things I don't know. I happened to be behind a door and I jumped him before he could pull the trigger, but it might as well have worked out another way. Fred Milburn was killed because he knew it couldn't have been Sam Harris who robbed the bank. But who did, Petey?"

"I'll reveal that in my own time, on my own terms."

"Petey," Shayne said, more and more exasperated with the little man. "Don't you have even the faintest inkling of the jam you're in? And we're both in the same boat, in more ways than one. I'll try to help you, God knows why, but we don't have any chance at all unless you level with me. Who pulled the Beach Trust job?"

"Don't tell me there's something the great private eye doesn't know?"

"Petey, will you forget that old feud for once? Forget about who's going to get the credit. We've got to use our heads, and take advantage of any break that comes up. What's the tie-in with the Truckers?"

"It'll be a long, cold day when I answer any questions you ask me, Shayne. You'll try to help! What a joke. I know what you think of me—you wouldn't throw water on me if I was on fire. You're trying to find out how much I know so you can tell your newfound friends. They couldn't get anything out of me any other way, so they rung you in. And as for somebody shooting at Rose, or killing that no-good con Milburn, I don't believe that for a minute. How could anybody kill him? He's in jail."

"Am I working for hoods or not?" Shayne said angrily. "If I am, I wouldn't have to ask you any questions. I'd know the answers."

"Maybe you don't know every last detail. This wouldn't be the first time in your life you've tried to play both ends against the middle. But you won't come out on top this time. You can whistle for that recovery fee. I'm enjoying this," he said, his tone contradicting the words. "I really am."

Shayne made a sound that was only half a word. He took a step forward, towering over the dishevelled figure on the bunk. "I've seen you do some moronic things, but you're surpassing yourself. It's between you and me now."

"Don't you dare lay a finger on me!"

"I'm going to lay more than my finger on you if you don't answer some questions. What did Plato have to do with the robbery?"

"Plato?" Painter smiled unpleasantly. "Not a thing that I know of."

Shayne reached out for him as the door opened. The small man named Gray walked in briskly. Jack Klipstone followed. The third man, the husky one with the tattooes, blocked the doorway. Painter looked past the redhead, and when he saw Gray his face changed.

"Gray! It's about time."

"Is it?" Gray said.

"I knew you'd show up sooner or later. They've been treating me like dirt, but I kept telling myself not to worry. The Senate was on their trail. This man Shayne is under arrest. Watch yourself with him. He can be tricky."

Gray smiled at Shayne. "Tricky, eh? What's wrong with your friend here, been hitting the sauce?"

"Oh, you know him, do you?" Painter said. "Well, I hope you brought enough cops with you, because there's one thing I learned about Shayne, he doesn't like to be arrested."

"I can understand that," Gray said cheerfully. "I'm like that myself."

"They certainly did a good job on you." Painter said, peering at him more closely. "Nobody would ever know your head had been cut open."

Gray touched his head and looked at his hand for traces of blood. "They cut me open? My, my. I hope they didn't take out anything I need. Here's the late news, men. You're making too much noise here, and we're going to tape you up. You first, Shayne."

Klipstone advanced on Shayne.

"He's one of the hoodlums, Gray!" Painter cried. "Grab him."

Gray laughed. Looking at Shayne, he tapped his temple meaningfully. "What next? Pink elephants?"

Painter said, confused, "You mean you aren't— Well, I'll say this, you look just like him!"

"When will you smarten up, Petey?" Shayne said. "Get it through your head—you've been conned."

"Conned?"

Gray went on laughing. "Put him out of his misery, Shayne."

"Listen to me, meat-head," Shayne said roughly. "At least you had the sense to know what you were doing was dangerous. You took on a bodyguard. The people who grabbed you had to get him out of the way, and they couldn't just invite you to get into their car and come along for the ride. They knew you'd act even more irrationally than usual if you thought you could hang something on me. Your views on the subject of Mike Shayne are in the public domain. Gray faked something. I don't know what. You called an ambulance for him and ordered an all-cars alert for me. Somebody fired a couple of shots to get Heinemann away from your Caddy. You saw a car that looked like mine and took out after it."

"You were in it! I saw you."

"Maybe you saw somebody that looked like me. You didn't see me." Shayne gauged Klipstone's height and build. Both were about right. So was his haircut, though he had brown hair. "What did you use, Jack? A henna rinse or a wig?"

Klipstone moved his feet, embarrassed. "Put your goddam hands behind you and turn around."

Shayne looked from one man to another. Gray had his hand inside his coat.

"Conscious or unconscious?" Gray said.

Shayne turned slowly, putting his hands together at the base of his spine.

"The filing cabinet!" Painter said desperately. "The way everything was thrown around. And the car, the car!"

Klipstone ripped off a length of tape and wrapped it around Shayne's wrists.

Gray said, "A car wouldn't be much of a problem, Chief. We didn't actually go to the trouble of stealing Shayne's car. There are plenty of cars like it, and we didn't want him to come out and notice it was missing. It's simpler to switch plates. People don't check to see whether they have the right plates from one week to the next. When it was all over, we switched the plates back. And the mess? How long would it take to straighten that up? Not very long. The timing was a bit off. I'd rather you hadn't called the ambulance and so on. But I couldn't stop you. Probably the phone should have been pulled out of the wall, but you can't think of everything."

Painter exclaimed, "That's the slimiest trick I ever heard of!"

Klipstone gave Shayne a push, tripping him. He fell heavily. After taping the redhead's ankles and slapping an X of tape across his mouth, he turned to Painter.

"Next."

"But—but I thought you were just going to leave me at a motel! You aren't actually—"

"It gets light in another hour," Gray said. "People show up to go out sailing, and we don't want you to yell for help and interfere with other people's recreation. If anybody asked me, I'd say take both of you out in the Stream and drop you, but nobody's asked me. Hands behind you, Chief."

"But—but—" Painter sputtered.

Klipstone plastered tape over his mouth before fastening his wrists and ankles. They went out and left Painter and Shayne alone. The key turned in the lock.

Shayne struggled into a sitting position, his back to the bulkhead. Painter lay on his side in the bunk. They looked at each other. Painter's eyes turned away evasively, but they kept coming back.

16

THE OVERLIGHT LIGHT had been left on. Painter seemed to be trying desperately to say something. As for the redhead, he wasn't interested in anything Painter had to say, and he had nothing to say himself that wouldn't have been profane.

Someone came down the companionway and went into the opposite cabin. There were footsteps and low voices overhead. After a time their captors settled down and the boat was quiet. Painter's eyes closed. He forced them open. But the next time they closed, several minutes later, they stayed closed. Shayne remained awake, his thoughts going in circles, like mice in a cage.

His watch was behind him, strapped up beneath overlapping layers of adhesive tape. The sky, which could be seen through the single porthole, was beginning to brighten. Dawn could be no more than fifteen minutes away. Exactly twenty-four hours earlier, he had parked his car in front of his hotel, and Joe Wing and his boys had moved in on him. And too much had happened in the next twenty-four hours that he didn't understand.

Occasionally he heard a car pass on the Beach, or the beat of a motor out in the bay. By now the fast Coast Guard cutters would have given up the search for the skin-diving bomber. Tim Rourke, he hoped, was still working north along the bayfront, looking for a large white boat called Panther. Unfortunately, he was also looking for a large white boat with a tuna-fish platform, but perhaps he would remember in time that such platforms are detachable.

Another boat's motor, louder than those he had heard so far, was approaching the marina, coming down from the north. His attention sharpened. It didn't go by, but swung into the open water between the lines of berthed boats, throttling down until it was barely turning over. Suddenly, no more than a half-cable length away, it cut out entirely. Shayne rocked forward, working his feet underneath him, and listened intently. He heard the faint slapping of waves against a hull; the other boat must be almost alongside.

Suddenly bare feet hit the deck directly overhead. Klipstone's voice called, "Who's that?"

When there was no answer a door slammed open across the companionway and someone ran up the companion ladder.

Klipstone's voice, low and worried, said, "It looks like Juan Grimondi. Get Gray." Then he called, "Juan? What gives, kid? Up late or up early?"

A voice with a strong Spanish accent answered, "Coming aboard you, Jack. Gotta talk about something."

Shayne heard someone else run out on the Panther's deck, and Gray said easily, "Take it easy, Juan, boy. You've got to be asked. That's one of the things about boats."

Shayne strained to hear the answer.

"Asked? You kidding me, boy. This here is important union business."

"But this ain't no union hall," Gray said softly. "Who you got there with you? Is that you, Whitey?" he called more challengingly. "I didn't know they let you out."

"I made parole," a voice answered from the other boat.

"And does your parole officer know you're this far from Baltimore? How many more you've got there, Juan? You brought a little army with you, didn't you? Hold it! We don't want to overload. We're crowded already."

Shayne pressed his back to the bulkhead and slowly began to work himself to his feet. On deck, the argument continued.

Juan said, "What's wrong with a little talk? We're good union brothers."

"I said, I said!" Grimondi said angrily. "I said so they let me get aboard. This is Plato's boat, right? Plato's boys snatched him. The cops find him and Shayne dead on Plato's boat, nobody's gonna bother with Luke, get it?"

"That's just like Luke," the other man said admiringly. "Smart."

They clattered up the steps. Shayne leaned forward and worked the tape off his ankles. It came readily. Painter was saying, "Wha—wha—" through the loose tape across his mouth. When Shayne's tape was off, he removed Painter's. The little man demanded angrily, "What are they doing?"

"Scuttling the boat," Shayne said in a fierce whisper. "Now shut up."

"I certainly will not! Scuttling the boat! It so happens I can't swim."

"Don't worry. I'll hold onto you."

"No," Painter said. "No, no, no. Absolutely not!" He pushed Shayne out of the way and started for the door. "Any time I let myself be rescued by *you*—"

Shayne overtook him in one long stride and pulled him around. Painter opened his mouth to yell, but Shayne brought his fist up in a crisp disciplinary punch. Painter's eyes turned up and his knees sagged. Shayne dumped him unceremoniously on the table. He opened the door to the companionway and listened.

"Find it?" the Cuban said on deck.

Another voice called from the engine room. "Water coming in to beat hell!"

Shayne could feel the difference in the trim of the boat. Whitey's voice asked, "What do we do with Klipstone?"

"Take him," the Cuban said. "And Whizzer. Luke can use them."

The Panther was settling fast. Shayne picked up the unconscious Painter and walked him to the door. He lifted him to get him past Gray's body, and as he did so, Painter's head snapped forward. He opened his mouth to complete the yell he had started before Shayne punched him. Shayne held his fist in front of his eyes, and he closed his mouth again, giving the redhead a look of extreme hatred. Shayne kept a firm grip on him as they went up the stairs.

"Going fast!" the Cuban cried. "Untie!"

Shayne kicked off his shoes. He couldn't take off his pants without letting go of Painter, whose eyes were darting in panic from one side of the companionway to the other. The boat lurched sharply to starboard. Shayne held Painter on the step next to the top, restraining him from running out on deck.

"No!" Painter cried clearly. "Let me—"

Shayne clapped his hand over the little man's mouth. "Do that again," he whispered, "and we'll both be killed."

Whitey's voice called from the other boat, "Did you hear that, Juan? Somebody—"

"Nah," the Cuban said scornfully. "Start up the motor."

The Panther righted herself for an instant, but her decks were awash. Shayne started to count. He got as far as six, and then the boat seemed to rush away beneath his feet. He had to use both hands to hold Painter, who was struggling like a cat being drowned. Water poured in through the companion doorway. Shayne thrust Painter ahead of him and pushed off hard.

They rode the bubbles to the surface. Shayne had one hand around Painter's mouth. He stroked hard with the other arm, coming up at an angle in the hope of being beneath the dock when they surfaced. But Painter was fighting too hard, and he didn't quite make it. Their heads broke water. He heard a cry from the Cuban's boat, and at the same instant, a siren.

He rolled on his side, shifting his grip to Painter's chin, and pulled hard for the dock. Painter floundered behind him, trying to get his arms around Shayne's neck. Shayne held him at arm's length. His wet clothes slowed him down, but he reached the dock before anyone on the Cuban's boat could get out a gun. Four more swift strokes carried him beneath the cross-walk. There were two sirens now, coming fast. The engine of the Cuban's boat was idling. Shayne noted the name on the stern as it swung toward him. Someone shouted in Spanish.

"Gotta get him!" Juan shouted. "Or Luke—"

"Hell with Luke," somebody answered. "Those are cops."

"Cops, cops. Hold it right here, or by God I knock you out of the boat with this forty-five."

Shayne pushed Painter against a piling. He heard the Cuban's feet on the cross-walk.

"Hang on," he whispered.

Painter reached for him desperately as he swam away, then snatched at the piling, wrapping both arms and legs around it. Shayne surface-dived silently and breast-stroked toward the Cuban's boat. He groped ahead of him in the black water. When his fingers touched a piling, he surfaced slowly, easing up to avoid a splash.

He heard the voice from the boat, low but penetrating, "Juan, they're coming, they're coming."

The Cuban made a sharp sound above Shayne, five feet toward the shore. Shayne moved quietly past the piling, grazing it lightly with his fingertips. He saw something move on the water—a long pointing shadow. Juan was leaning far down, his gun ready, watching and listening intently. Shayne sank beneath the surface, turned in the Cuban's direction and planted his feet solidly against the piling. He straightened his knees, kicking backward, and shot upward through the water.

He had misjudged his distance slightly, but as he flashed into the open he changed direction with a powerful flip of his body. His hand fastened on the Cuban's arm. He heard a shout from the boat. The Cuban grunted and tried to turn the gun, but he was half over the edge, and his balance was wrong. Shayne twisted, kicking, and dragged the Cuban into the water.

He took him down, concentrating on the gun. The Cuban stabbed at Shayne's face with the rigid fingers of his free hand. Shayne's legs scissored around the Cuban's waist. Still they went down. Shayne had filled his lungs before he attacked, but the Cuban had been caught by surprise. Another moment, and he was no longer trying to hurt Shayne, but to get away.

They were down in muddy water, roiled by the settling of Plato's boat. The Cuban dropped the gun and clawed upward. Instantly Shayne pushed toward the surface. The Cuban hit at him when they broke water. Shayne clipped him behind the ear, but not hard enough to stun him. He continued to struggle. Shayne tried to maneuver him around to get a clear shot at a knockout point, but his arms and legs were heavy and the frantic Cuban was as hard to control as a fighting salmon. Shayne pushed him back against the nearest piling and banged his head until he felt the lithe body go limp in his hands.

Men were running out on the dock. The Cuban's boat swung out into the bay, its throttle opened up full. Shayne towed the Cuban to where he had left Painter. For a minute he thought the little man had let go, choosing to drown himself in preference to being saved by Michael Shayne.

"Painter!" he shouted. "Goddamn it—"

But he had made a mistake in the half light. He saw Painter clinging to the next piling.

"I'm never going to forget this, I warn you!" Painter said. "You deliberately let them sink that boat. You thought you were going to get rid of me, didn't you?"

Suddenly Shayne was filled with cold fury. "You got yourself into this all by yourself, and I wish I'd let you get out of it. You found some evidence that would save a man from execution. It must have been pure luck, but you found it. And then you held it up so you'd get more personal publicity out of it. You fell for the oldest dodge in the book, you were so goddam anxious to get something on me—"

"And I'll get it yet, don't worry!"

"Who really robbed the Beach Trust, Petey? Luke Quinn?"

Painter howled. "No, you don't! You think you can grab the spotlight now, after everything I've gone through? No, sir. I'm way ahead of you."

Shayne suppressed an impulse to drag him into the water. "Have it your own way," he said wearily.

"And don't you forget it!"

The dock above them reverberated to the sound of footsteps. Tim Rourke's voice called, "Mike Shayne, are you down there?"

His head appeared upside down at the edge of the dock. A gun went off, but the escaping boat was beyond pistol-range. Other heads appeared beside Tim's, and one of the cops played a flashlight into the shadows. Shayne swam toward the light, towing the Cuban. Rourke reached down, Shayne reached up and their hands joined.

"I called the cops when I found your car," Rourke said. "That's not the Panther out there. What the hell happened?"

Other hands came down and dragged Shayne and the Cuban out of the water.

"And that's not Petey!" Rourke exclaimed.

A voice sounded faintly from beneath the dock. "What do you bastards think you're doing? Get a rope down here or you're going to be back walking a beat, the lot of you, and by God, I mean it!"

Rourke made a face. "Stupid of me, I know. But I was kind of hoping he might be different."

17

TIM ROURKE RACED back to his car, returning with a Japanese camera loaded with fast film. He arrived just as one of the cops was reaching down for Painter. But Painter hated to relinquish his grip on the piling, and the cop couldn't quite touch his chief's outstretched fingers until Shayne and a second cop held him by the legs. Rourke was ready. As Painter came over the side, sputtering, Rourke made the picture, which appeared on the front page of that day's *News*.

"Get that man!" Painter yelled. "Confiscate his camera!"

Then his eye fell on Shayne. "I thought you'd be a couple of miles from here by now. Arrest this man. If he gives you any trouble, put the cuffs on him."

"Arrest me for what?" Shayne said quietly. "Assaulting an investigator for a Senate Committee?"

"No," Painter said. "For—for—" he looked around. "For—"

"Petey, don't you think you better put out a call for that boat? Her name's Ophelia, and her home port's Baltimore, in case you were under water at the time and didn't notice. We'll be in better shape if we can pick them up before they get to a phone."

"I'm capable of giving the orders around here, thank you. Get out a call for the Ophelia," he said sternly. "From—" He looked at Shayne.

"Baltimore," Shayne said. "Heading down the bay."

One of the cops ran toward his radio, and Painter looked down at the Cuban, who was conscious but not yet active. "Let me see, which one is this?"

"His name's Juan Grimondi," Shayne told him. "He works for Luke Quinn. He was driving for the guy who tried to shoot Rose Heminway yesterday morning. He killed one of Plato's thugs, named Gray. On top of that, he's just committed piracy."

Painter's mouth was open. "He did? Yeah. Okay, book him."

He started away, managing a good imitation of his usual cocky strut, in spite of the flapping garter. Rourke said in a low voice to Shayne, "I didn't believe it at first. The son of a bitch is loaded."

As though to prove it, Painter veered toward the edge of the dock. One of the cops grabbed him to keep him from falling in.

"I feel dizzy all of a sudden," Painter said, and sneezed so hard he almost jolted himself out of the cop's hands.

"What you need is a shot, Chief," the cop said solicitously. "You're catching cold. I always carry a pint in the car, for emergencies."

Shayne and Rourke exchanged a look and hurried after them, leaving the third cop to bring the Cuban. In front of the clubhouse, the cop pulled open the door of the prowl sedan, and produced a pint of blended whiskey. Painter took it in both hands and drank eagerly.

"None for you," he said, noticing Shayne. "Not after the way you hogged the liquor on the boat." He sneezed again. "I've got to get into some dry clothes, and then we're going to raise a little hell in a certain union."

"Petey!" Shayne said brusquely, holding the door so it wouldn't close. "I know it's asking a lot, but think. As far as they know, you're at the bottom of the bay. Let's use it. You're behind the times. Things have happened since the night before last."

"I'll catch up," Painter said.

"How did you get on Quinn's trail in the first place? You found something in Benjamin Chadwick's wallet, isn't that right? Okay, where is it now?"

"Take off," Painter told the cop at the wheel. "If you have to run over any private detectives, don't hesitate." He swivelled back to Shayne, and made an anguished stab at his breast pocket. "It's—"

"You're damn right it's gone," Shayne grated. "The people who picked you up weren't working for Quinn, but for Plato. Naturally they searched you. Naturally they'd be glad to find something they could use to hold over Quinn. Is your mind finally working? Go ahead and walk in and arrest Quinn, in front of the TV cameras. How long do you think you can hold him?"

"I can hold him," Painter said unconvincingly. "I've got a very strong case, and I have no intention of giving it away to you."

"What's this strong case consist of? Chadwick can't talk. Milburn's dead. You've got one thing, and that's all. Just before the robbery, Quinn was in hock to a loan shark. Just after the robbery he was able to pay off the loan shark and buy enough votes to move up in the union. That could be the cincher if you had anything else, but it's not enough by itself."

Painter sank back in the seat, seeming suddenly much smaller than usual. "I went through all this for nothing. I damn near drowned—"

"It's not as bad as that. They're fighting among themselves, and to take advantage of it we've got to work together. This can be a big thing for you, Petey. You can have the TV screen all to yourself. I'll be satisfied with a small check from the insurance company."

"As usual," Painter said bitterly.

"As usual, and I think I deserve it. What time are they holding the election?" Shayne asked Rourke, who was standing beside him listening avidly.

"That's their first order of business," Rourke said, "and

they've got the Honest Ballot Association to make the count. We'd better get moving, Mike," he added nervously. "The *Herald's* going to have a man here any minute."

"It's your story, Tim," Shayne said. "Painter and I would probably both be dead now if you hadn't called the cops."

He looked at his watch. It was supposed to be waterproof, but it had been through too much violent activity in the last half hour, and was no longer running.

Rourke said, "Just before seven, Mike."

"That gives us time enough, if it doesn't take Petey more than an hour to tell us what he found in Benjamin Chadwick's wallet."

Painter sighed heavily. "How did you know—"

Looking down at him, Shayne said, "That's when you put on a bodyguard. When somebody collapses on your doorstep, you look in his wallet for his name and address. You found that, and you also found something else."

"A picture," Painter said. "A 35 mm negative. I had it developed, and there was Luke Quinn, looking straight at the camera. He had a suitcase in one hand, and he was coming out of a vault."

"Great detective work," Shayne said sarcastically. "I knew it had to be something simple. No, I take that back, Petey," he added quickly. "Now that we're working together I've got to start being polite."

"Maybe I should have turned it over to the FBI and let them make the arrest," Painter said. "But why let somebody else in on it when I'm the one who— And there's no reason to look at me like that. Not everybody would have thought of developing that picture. I dug up the loan shark, I found Fred Milburn and I did a good job of worming the truth out of him, if I say it myself. Quinn was coming down to Miami for the convention, so why shouldn't I make the arrest myself? It was just a matter of a few days, a week at the most. Meanwhile, I could make it airtight. Well, I guess we all make mistakes."

Rourke and Shayne looked at each other in astonishment.

Neither had ever heard the little chief of detectives make any such admission before.

"That's all right, Petey," Rourke said soothingly. "You go home. You'll feel more like yourself when you've had some sleep."

"Sleep? This is no time for sleep."

He glanced at the driver, who was as surprised as the others at the turn the conversation was taking. Coming out of the car, Painter took Shayne's arm and drew him to the dock, where they wouldn't be overheard.

"What did you have in mind, Shayne? I'm not saying I'll do it, you understand. But it's perfectly true I've been out of circulation for a day. If you want to make a suggestion, I'll be glad to consider it."

Rourke followed Shayne's Buick to the redhead's apartment hotel. He phoned his paper while Shayne showered and shaved. Soon afterward a copy boy arrived to pick up his exposed film. The coffee was ready by the time Shayne was dressed. Shayne took a cup to the phone, where he made several calls. Meanwhile, Rourke was using his razor.

Shayne called from the phone, "Do you happen to know who writes the insurance for the Beach Trust? Wouldn't that be Acme?"

Rourke answered from the bathroom. "They get most of the business in that part of town. Who do you think's going to be there at this time of the morning?"

"Nobody. I'm calling the president, what's-his-name, Goddard. He'll be glad to skip breakfast."

Rourke finished shaving and combed his hair, using Shayne's equipment. The two men were more presentable when they were ready to leave.

"Wearing a hat, Mike?" Rourke said. "Isn't that overdoing it a little?"

"Who knows? We may be on TV."

"Gad. And I don't have any make-up on."

They pushed through the revolving door into the St. Albans lobby at five minutes of nine. From the number of police cars parked outside, Shayne saw that Painter had completed his part of the arrangements. Rose Heminway hurried across the lobby.

"Michael! I honestly don't think I can stand much more of this. Is this how you live all the time?"

"Not quite," Shayne said. "Sometimes I get a little sleep."

They walked up one flight to the ballroom. Rourke used his press-pass, and Shayne and Rose went up another half-flight to the gallery. They found seats overlooking a scene of considerable disorder. Harry Plato, on the dais, was hammering vainly with his gavel, but the delegates were in no hurry to settle down. One end of the gallery had been taken over by the TV cameras, which were not yet turned on. Rourke slipped into an empty chair at the press table, below Plato's microphone.

"Take your places, brothers," Plato was shouting. "This convention will come to order."

Luke Quinn emerged from one of the side rooms, surrounded by a compact group of ten or twelve men, all but one of whom were smoking cigars. He said something to one of the men, and that man and several of the others laughed.

"Isn't that Luke Quinn?" Rose remarked. "He wasn't this sure of himself when I knew him."

Gradually the knots of delegates broke up and drifted to seats at the long tables, which seemed to be arranged by geographical districts. Shayne glanced at his watch, which was functioning again. He saw Goddard, the insurance company president, come into the gallery and look around until he saw Shayne. The redhead gave him an inquisitive glance. He nodded.

"Wait here, Rose," Shayne said. "I'll want you later, so don't go anywhere."

He returned to the main floor, passing a compact formation of fifteen or twenty uniformed cops, and went along the hall to the entrance nearest the dais. Plato had brought the convention to order and a minister was giving the invocation. Shayne doubted if many of the delegates were actually praying. He was stopped at the door by a burly sergeant-at-arms. He found an envelope in his pocket and borrowed a pencil. Holding the envelope against the wall, he wrote: "Harry, Did you know the Panther has been sunk with all hands?—Shayne."

He folded the envelope and gave it to the sergeant-at-arms with a five-dollar bill. "Hand this up to Harry."

"After he gets done?"

"Now."

The man gave the envelope to someone at the nearest table, who passed it across the aisle. The minister finished the invocation and sat down. Shayne watched his message travel from table to table until it was finally passed up to Plato, who was back at the microphone. He finished a sentence and glanced at what Shayne had written. He went on, but broke into the next sentence and read the note again. He looked across at Shayne, who was planted in the doorway, his hat pushed back on his head, his hands in his pockets. Shayne grinned. After a moment Plato called another official to take the gavel, and came down. The ballroom was reasonably quiet, and the delegates were all watching him. His eyes were stormy.

As he came up to Shayne, the redhead said pleasantly, "I thought I'd be telling you something you didn't know."

"In private, baby," Plato said briefly.

He led the way to a door marked, *Midwest*. He called over a nearby lounger. "We don't want to be bothered in here."

"Sure, Harry."

They entered a private dining room, which was being used as headquarters of the Midwest district. A secretary was drinking coffee from a cardboard container.

"Outside," Plato said.

"Certainly," she said, spilling some of the coffee.

She went out hurriedly. Shayne tossed his hat on the nearest desk and sat down on the desk beside it. "Where do you keep your liquor?"

"Let's do it without," Plato said. He picked up the phone, put it in a bottom drawer and stuffed rags around it. "We go over the place for bugs a couple of times a day, and we keep finding them, too. But with a phone you never know until you take it apart."

Shayne grinned. "You don't mean people want to listen to your private conversations?"

"Mike, you don't know. They're thicker than seagulls around a garbage scow, at convention time especially. Thank the Lord I had the sense to get out of it. Say it fast because I got to get out to vote for myself."

"The water's probably not over fifteen feet deep where she went down, Harry, so you can raise her. But let's talk about money for a minute. I could use a retainer."

"I might arrange something, Mike. In how many figures?"

"I keep thinking of about a thousand a month."

Plato looked at him closely. "You're trying to tell me it's serious?"

"Yeah," Shayne said soberly.

Plato cracked one powerful fist into his other palm, and for a long moment he did nothing but swear, using language he had learned before he became a labor statesman.

"You take the words out of my mouth," Shayne said.

"What I'd like to do to that son of a bitch! Well, I better get the details on it so I don't make a mistake."

"You don't want to hear the whole thing, Harry. I was looking for Painter. I—"

Plato raised a hand, puzzled. "I thought you two had a grudge fight going. What's that, something they made up to sell papers?"

Shayne smiled. "There's *something* to it. But he was planning to break a story yesterday morning, and I was looking for him to find out what it was. I found out. Do you know a hood named Juan Grimondi? And an ex-con from Baltimore, called Whitey?"

Plato ran his hand across his jaw. "Those names seem to ring a bell."

"There were eight or nine in all. Your boys put up a good scrap, but they were outclassed. Gray's dead."

"Yeah?" Plato said bleakly. "I'm sorry to hear it. He was a good man."

"That's about all I can tell you. They opened up a plate in the engine room and she went down fast. Painter was taped up in a locked cabin, and I've got mixed feelings about that. It's bad for public morality when one of you people knock over a cop. All things being equal, I'd like to put somebody away for it. But all things aren't equal. A grand a month that I won't have to pay taxes on is quite an inducement."

Plato waited a moment, the fingers of his right hand opening and closing. "Jesus, I'll be lucky to get out of this without a bleeding ulcer. It's a deal, Shayne, as of now. The first thing I'd like to have you do is bring that son of a bitch in here."

Shayne got off the desk. "Quinn? What do I say to him?"

Plato smiled grimly. "I'm still president of this goddam union, for another half hour. Do you carry a gun, Shayne?"

"No. Do I need one?"

"It might be a good idea, for when Quinn realizes you saw the Panther go down. I don't think he'll try to pull anything here, we got just about every cop in town, but the bastard is crazy! He's out of his mind! Take care of your health, would be my advice."

"I'll do it for your sake, Harry," Shayne told him. "So long as I'm healthy you've *really* got something to use on Quinn."

"I'm thinking of that," Plato said.

Shayne went out, leaving the union president slumped in an armchair, looking old. The redhead used the door where the sergeant-at-arms knew him. The balloting was about to begin. There were two voting machines, and officials of the Honest Ballot Association were ready with delegate rosters, to be sure that no faction tried to vote its men more than once. The TV cameras were recording the scene, but neither cameraman bothered to follow the tall, rangy figure of Michael Shayne as he made his way among the tables and up to Quinn.

Quinn's after-breakfast cigar had burned down halfway. The smell of tobacco mingled with the strong smell of after-shaving lotion. He was tipped back slightly in the chair, giving off an atmosphere of power and confidence, but Shayne saw that his manicured fingers were drumming nervously against his leg.

"Quinn?" Shayne said.

Quinn looked at him coldly through his horn-rimmed glasses. "We got a rule against letting private dicks on the floor."

"They waived it for me," Shayne said, "and it only cost me five bucks. Harry wants to see you."

"Here I am," Quinn said indifferently. "He knows what I look like."

Shayne smiled down at him. "He also knows what you looked like three years ago, when you still owed Sticky Horvath some money."

"Christ," Quinn said in his gravelly voice, and added for the benefit of his fellow-delegates, who were pretending not to listen, "He probably needs somebody to tie his shoelaces. He's on his way down, and we're all as sorry as we can be. Hell, he's got another twenty-five minutes, let him live it up."

The delegate beside him said, "What do we do about—you know, the Welfare Fund?"

"Plenty of time," Quinn said. "They'll keep the machines open till everybody votes."

He came with Shayne. Outside in the corridor he started to speak, but straightened his glasses instead and walked on, puffing busily at his cigar.

"You working for Harry these days?"

"He made me an offer," Shayne said, "but I'm not sure he has much of a future."

"Now that's using the head, Shayne. I'll give you a tip. He hasn't got *any* future."

Plato was standing, facing the door. He had succeeded in summoning up his old belligerent expression.

Shayne said, "You won't want me, will you, Harry?"

"Stand by outside. Nobody comes in. Nobody."

Shayne closed the door and moved fast. He called to the nearest cop. "Nobody in or out of this door," he said, echoing Plato.

Lieutenant Wing was coming toward him. Shayne signalled, and Wing met him at the entrance Shayne had used before.

"Wait a minute," the sergeant-at-arms said.

Shayne went on to the press table and worked in beside Rourke.

"It's all set, Mike," Rourke said in a low voice.

Shayne looked at the floor. The reporter had hooked into the main cable from the microphone, scraping off the insulation and tying in two wires from a small receiving set in his lap.

"I thought I was going to take a few thousand volts doing it," he said. "But how did you plant the mike? Wasn't he with you all the time?"

"It's in my hat," Shayne said. "The hat's out on a desk. We ought to get good reception."

"Son of a bitch," Rourke commented.

Wing sent two cops to stand beside the microphone above them. Shayne switched on the receiver. It was a powerful set, manufactured for this purpose and no other. It only received on one wave-length and its single knob was a volume-control. There was a good deal of noise in the hall, but Shayne heard a faint crackling from the loud-speakers suspended from each corner of the gallery. He grinned at Rourke and stepped up the volume.

Plato's voice roared over the public address: "When are you going to get it through your thick head that times have changed?"

18

THE GENERAL BABBLE in the ballroom was cut off as abruptly as if it were controlled by a single switch. Everyone looked toward the dais, where the two cops stood self-consciously on either side of the unattended mike. Shayne turned the knob, and Plato's voice continued more quietly: "If you think you can get away with that kind of rough stuff, you're making a mistake, Luke. The newspapers. The goddam Senate."

Quinn replied with a truck-driver's obscenity, telling Plato what the Senate could do, and it came over clearly.

Rourke said, "I wonder if that went over the TV."

"The country may survive," Shayne said.

Plato repeated the obscenity sarcastically. "I wish they could hear you say that. All right, kid, how you planning to swing in the vote?"

"I have respect for you, Harry," Quinn said. "You did a lot for this union. And you did a lot for yourself too, not to speak of your family and your wife's family, but let's not talk about that. I hate to break it to you this way. We're dumping you. You get the pension, and that's all."

Plato's voice was hard. "You're going for that—that—"

"We're going for your distinguished opponent from San Francisco. And you're speaking of the future president of the Welfare Fund, so watch your language. I listened to the offers. We talked it over. And when I saw a way to take care of this Painter situation, I put the word around—what we need in the leadership is some representation from the West Coast."

In the ballroom, the voting had stopped. The delegates had

formed in lines leading to the tables to have their credentials checked, but the lines weren't moving. Several of the most burly delegates moved toward the microphone. Wing's reserves formed, two deep, nightsticks ready. For an instant it looked as though the TV cameras would record some real action, but the threat fell apart before it reached the police line.

Shayne called to Wing, "Put another half dozen men in front of the Midwest office, Joe."

"What did they offer you?" Plato cried. "Human blood?"

Quinn replied calmly, "I've got his promise for two years from now."

"For what?" Plato was almost screaming, and Shayne turned down the volume. "For *president?* You want to step into my shoes?"

"Not right away, Harry. I'm not ready. Two years from now we figure will be about right."

Plato said, "I knew you were crazy. You don't have the—the stature, Luke. Everybody knows it. And your background! You're vulnerable."

"Not any more," Quinn said.

"You're wide open! I got this union finally a little respectable, and how's it going to look when the international president's put away for murder?"

"I'm in the clear, Harry. Not all the way in the clear, but close enough. I've got two years to take care of everything."

"No, Luke, it can't be done. You left too many loose ends. We're in the goddam limelight, you can't do things the old way. Sending goons to knock off that girl! That's crude, Luke. You solve one problem and you make a couple more. Knocking off Milburn, okay, that's the one thing you handled right. I think I'd even let you get away with knocking off Painter, because the dumb little no-good had it coming. But I'll be damned"—his voice thickened—"if I'm going to let you get away *sinking my boat!*"

"I asked you to hand him over, Harry. I had to take him."

"I had him under control."

"And for how long? You found out what he was working

on, I don't know who from. That crumb Horvath, probably. Yeah, and he's somebody else who's going to get it in the head. And did you tell me so I could take care of it? You did not. You grabbed Painter and put him in the freezer so he couldn't blow the whistle on me till you had both fists in the Welfare Fund. That may be good politics, but it's not so hot, friendship-wise. I can't feel so warm to you any more. And after the election? You were going to get him found with a babe in a motel, I hear! You'd have the Fund. And me? I'd change places with Sam Harris in condemned row."

"That's the risk you run when you kill people," Plato said.

The TV cameras had discovered the receiver in front of Rourke. The reporter straightened his tie self-consciously.

Quinn's gravelly voice went on, "It was an accident. I had to shoot Heminway, Harry. Nobody was supposed to be there that night. He loomed up in front of me, and I had to blast him."

"Sure, sure," Plato said. "I forgive you. But will the State of Florida forgive you? What I don't understand is why you posed for a picture."

Shayne leaned forward to hear the answer.

"That bastard Ben Chadwick," Quinn's voice said. "The bank president. He set it on automatic, with infra-red so I never knew it went off. He wanted to make sure I wouldn't go light on his end of the split. And when I saw a print of that picture, believe me, I handed over every last buck he deserved."

Rourke's eyebrows went up. "I smell a recovery fee, you dog."

Standing up, Shayne motioned to Goddard in the balcony. He pointed toward the exit, and the insurance company president nodded. Shayne gave Rose Heminway the same sign, accompanying it with a hurry-up motion.

Plato said, "We're wasting time. I'll tell you what I want you to do—go out and tell your people that Harry Plato's the man."

Quinn laughed unpleasantly. "Give up, Harry. So long as

you had Painter hanging over me I had to take your advice. But not any more."

"I'm not forgetting how that happened, either," Plato said. "I'll send a diver down to get him, so I can dump him somewhere else, but I'm not forgetting you figured he'd be found on my boat. That was dirty pool, Luke, and you're going to pay for it."

"Tell me how," Quinn said.

"I'll be glad to," Plato answered carelessly. "I've got the picture."

Shayne nodded to Rourke. "They'll be yelling at each other in a minute. Let's break it up."

Quinn, at the other end of the transmission, whispered, "You've got the picture?"

"Of you coming out of the vault, just before George Heminway came around the corner. Chadwick had it with him the day he flopped on Painter's front steps. I got it from Painter."

"You mean he was *carrying it around?*"

"That's Painter," Plato said. "Brains aren't his big feature. Naturally *I'm* not dumb enough to carry it around, so you can put that gun back in your pocket."

A door came open violently, and Peter Painter's voice cried over the public address: "So brains aren't my big feature, are they?"

"Pa-painter!" Quinn said.

"I don't blame you for stuttering," Painter said with satisfaction. "You thought you could get the better of me, did you?"

Shayne jerked his head toward the exit. Rourke came with him, hurrying to keep ahead of the other reporters and wire agency men. Rose Heminway and Goddard were waiting in the corridor. Shayne swept them along with him to the open door of the Midwest office. Rourke managed to be last.

"Nobody else," he told the cop, and closed the door behind him.

Shayne, two strides ahead of his friend, saw Luke Quinn with a big gun in his hand, pointing it at Painter. The barrel wavered as Shayne and the others thrust through the door. Rose gave a small scream.

"Don't move, goddam it," Quinn said. "Any of you."

Painter walked calmly up to him. Quinn swung the gun back, but Painter batted it aside with his left hand and hung a right on Quinn's jaw. As the blow landed the gun went off. To Shayne's surprise, Quinn sat down. Harry Plato kicked the gun out of his hand.

Painter turned toward the others. "Big, tough hoodlum," he sneered.

His eyes were bloodshot. He had tried to shave, but his jowls were cross-hatched with small cuts. A strong smell of gin hung in the air. As Shayne approached, the report of the gun registered on Painter's brain and he sagged into a chair.

"Get up," Shayne told Quinn.

Quinn's head lolled. Shayne gripped the front of his shirt. Heaving him erect, Shayne walked him to a leather sofa. Painter began to recover as he saw the effect of his roundhouse punch.

"When I hit them," he observed, "they stay hit."

Shayne shook Quinn's shoulders and slapped him sharply twice. "It's the end of the trail, Luke. You've had three years, but it's finished."

He picked up his hat from the desk and pulled out the little sending set. "These are wonderful gadgets. They cost an arm and a leg, but they're worth it. Everything you and Harry just said went out over the public address. The TV boys taped it and it'll go out to the country later, minus some of the profanity. Five hundred people heard you admit you robbed the Beach Trust and shot George Heminway. The Coast Guard picked up the Ophelia, with Grimandi and the rest of your people. Painter's alive, as you've just found out. Rose is alive. So is her father. I think Harry's going to turn that picture over to us so he'll win our friendship and we won't prosecute him for kidnapping. At this point he needs all the friends he can get."

"Mike—" Plato said weakly.

Shayne said, "Luke wants to clear up a few things for his friends in the ballroom first. Go ahead, Luke."

Quinn pulled himself together and repeated his earlier obscenity. Shayne made a reproving sound.

"Think about it, Luke. You don't want to be the only one who gets burned, do you? Of course you don't. Who had the idea for the robbery, you or Chadwick?"

Quinn looked around the room. Then he made up his mind and said viciously, "It sure as hell wasn't me. We had this deal going—collecting dough for the Red Cross, and he kept wailing about how he needed cash, he needed cash—"

"No," Rose breathed.

"Oh, yes," Quinn said more strongly. "I'm not going to take the jolt and let him hang onto that hundred and forty thousand I counted out in his lap. What *I* suggested, if he needed cash I suggested robbing the Red Cross, they'd never miss it, but Chadwick, he got up on his high horse. Rob the Red Cross! Who did I think I was talking to? I felt like a bum, and I was about to crawl out on my hands and knees when he said wait, he had a better idea, and this was it."

"You're lying!" Rose exclaimed.

Shayne cut her short with a gesture. "What was the split, Luke?"

"Down the middle, after expenses. I paid my debts, and laid out the rest so I got a nice advancement in the union, and everything was going fine till that Harris dame—I'd like to pull her apart!"

"What made you send a couple of gunmen to Rose?" Shayne said. "None of us liked that, Luke."

"I had to," he said reasonably. "She walked in on us, on Chadwick and me, when we were going over a layout of the bank. I don't know what she made of it, but if she ever started thinking about it, I'd be dead."

"I thought it was a map of the town," Rose said, appalled. "For the Red Cross campaign. It never entered my head—"

"Just a minute," Shayne said gently. "Milburn's stabbing, Luke. How did you arrange that?"

Quinn bared his teeth. "In front of all these people?"

Rourke suggested, "Let's turn off the radio, Mike. I want some of this exclusive."

Shayne clicked off the sending switch. "Now do you feel better, Luke?"

Quinn went on sneering. "You're the big brain here. You know all about it anyway."

"I can guess," Shayne said. "When Painter asked to see Milburn, they called him out of the mess-hall. A few hours later the warden put several of the prisoners' leaders on discipline. Everybody knows how simple it is to bludgeon a two-time loser into turning stool pigeon. I think we'll find some members of your local in jail. That doesn't mean any of them did the actual stabbing. Starting a good strong rumor would be enough."

"Now you're worrying me, Shayne," Quinn said.

"Do you ever do any skin-diving, Luke? That's something else we'll want to look into, to tidy everything up. It doesn't matter too much. You can't be executed more than once, and what you're going to be executed for is the murder of George Heminway . . . Where are you going, Rose?"

She turned. "Mike, hadn't I better call Norma Harris? It seems cruel to keep her in suspense."

"Her big interest is the money," Shayne said. "I'm coming to that."

"The money?"

"Sure. I wouldn't want you to keep it, when you're the one who sent your husband to the bank that night."

Painter sat up straighter. "Now look here, Mike. Just because you had a few lucky breaks doesn't entitle you to—"

"Right or wrong, Rose?" Shayne said.

"Wrong," she said coldly. "As wrong as you could possibly be."

Shayne smiled. "And how could we prove it, anyway? After three years, we probably can't even prove that your father was helping himself to the bank's assets even before you suggested the robbery to him. I really don't think he'd go into partnership with a character like Quinn unless he already had a shortage he couldn't cover."

"Sixty G's," Quinn said. "Or so he told me. Of course he wasn't George Washington, as far as telling the truth was concerned."

"That's the most—the most despicable—" Rose said.

"Well, Luke's a despicable character," Shayne said tolerantly. "I've been thinking about this, and I think I know about what happened. Your husband found out what his crooked father-in-law was up to. What's more natural than for a husband to confide in his understanding wife? But he made a mistake there, because you're the type of understanding wife that thinks things through. If George turned your old man in for embezzlement, he'd either go to jail or the bank would fire him and make him sell everything he owned to pay them back. Without a father-in-law at the head of the bank, George would stay at his adding machine for the rest of his career, and life as a clerk's wife, with a father to support, was not for you.

"I'd better not try to guess which of you actually thought up the robbery, you or your old man, and that's another thing that doesn't matter. But of course you knew about it. Luke wouldn't put thugs on you unless he was damn sure you knew everything there was to know about that night. When George came to you with his problem, you told him you couldn't believe it, you had to have proof, and that meant he had to go back to the bank and work late, on his own time, with nobody else around. He got the proof, all right, but from the wrong end of a gun."

She started to speak and he said cheerfully, "This is all guesswork. I admit it."

"When Norma came to me I did everything she wanted," she said. "I tried to push Mr. Painter—"

"No, you didn't," Shayne said. "You went to him to find out what he knew, if anything. Your father went to him for the same reason, and I think he may have wondered if you'd sold him out."

"But I—I hired you, Mike. Doesn't that prove—"

"You suddenly realized you needed protection. Luke Quinn, who was coming to town this week, was friends with some very rough men."

"Mike," she said quietly, "your tone's so—I don't know—so vindictive. I thought you—you and I—"

Shayne looked at her in surprise. "Just because you offered to sleep with me, you thought I'd let you keep the money? That's not the way I operate."

Rourke put in, "He's already got a girl."

Rose looked from Shayne to Painter. The chief-of-detectives looked away, flicking his thumbnail across his mustache. She seemed to harden as she saw that Shayne's reasoning had left her without allies.

"Just exactly what do you intend to do about it?"

"There's not much we can do," Shayne said. "You didn't fire the gun that killed your husband, Quinn did, and there's no way we can prove conspiracy. We can't even prove perjury on your identification of Harris—you had the sense to qualify that. But we can take the money away from you. Goddard," he said, addressing the insurance company president, "do you want to speak on that point?"

"I checked the banks for safe deposit accounts, as you asked me to," Goddard said. "There's one in Mrs. Heminway's name and one in her father's. It wouldn't have mattered if you'd let her leave a minute ago, Mike, because I put a temporary stop-order on those boxes until we can get court permission to see what's inside them. The Bay Harbor property ought to bring a nice price."

"It's not my father's!" Rose cried. "It's mine!"

"But he bought it for you, probably? It may take some litigation, but if Shayne's charges hold up, and having worked with Shayne before, I have a feeling they will, I think the courts will decide that it was bought with money that properly belongs to us. That would go for any other real property, bought since your husband's death. A car, say, jewelry, fur coats."

Rose looked confused. "I'll be left with nothing? Nothing at all?"

Painter said quickly, "You admit it?"

She rallied. "I don't admit a thing! You're going to have a fight on your hands! And as for you, Michael Shayne, I wish I'd paid more attention to the stories I've heard about you. You don't want to settle for my little fee. You're after higher stakes."

Shayne said soberly, "No, I'm charging you my usual rates, and I expect to get paid. I promised I'd give Sam Harris twenty-five percent of the recovery fee, but I've decided he deserves it all. He's spent three years in jail on a bad rap, and I doubt if the state of Florida will do anything but say they're sorry." He added to Rourke, "But don't tell Lucy about this, Tim."

"Norma Harris!" Rose exclaimed. "I might have known. That over-sexed, over-developed bitch. You're birds of a feather!"

Shayne grinned. "I'm giving it to Sam, not Norma. It may be just the thing to keep their marriage together."

"This isn't in character, Mike," Rourke observed. "Lucy wouldn't believe it even if I told her."

The door opened and a union official looked in. "Harry—"

He looked around, and Plato said impatiently, "Well? Hurry it up, because I've got to get out there and take the chair, if I'm going to hold the membership in line."

"They just announced the results, Harry. You ran third. The rank-and-file—"

"What?" Plato demanded.

"Well, they won, Harry, all down the line."

"We only put them on the ballot so there'd be a contest!" Plato cried. "What do those jerks know about running a union?" He turned angrily on Shayne. "And how about me? How about me? This is all your fault, you bastard. I've never been able to put aside a penny. I hope you're satisfied! I'll have to go back to driving a truck!"